THE WORKS OF ANATOLE FRANCE
IN AN ENGLISH TRANSLATION
EDITED BY THE LATE FREDERIC
CHAPMAN AND JAMES LEWIS MAY

ˉLITTLE PIERRE

LITTLE PIERRE
BY ANATOLE FRANCE

A TRANSLATION BY
J. LEWIS MAY

LONDON: JOHN LANE, THE BODLEY HEAD
NEW YORK: JOHN LANE COMPANY.·.MCMXX

Press of
J. J. Little & Ives Company
New York, U. S. A.

CONTENTS

LITTLE PIERRE

LITTLE PIERRE

CHAPTER I

Incipe, Parve Puer, Risu Cognoscere Matrem

Y mother often used to tell me a variety of things connected with my entry into this world that did not strike me as meriting the importance she attached to them. I paid no very great attention to them and they have faded from my recollection.

"Quand vient l'enfant à recevoir,
Il faut la sage-femme avoir
Et des commères un grand tas . . ."

It may certainly be affirmed, if the stories told me were true, that the custom referred to in these lines of an old Parisian rhymester had not altogether fallen into desuetude in the days when the reign of King Louis Philippe was drawing to a close; for there was a great gathering of worthy dames in Mistress Nozière's bedchamber to await my arrival in this vale of tears. It was April and the weather was chilly. Four or five of the neighbouring gossips, among them Madame Caumont, who had a bookshop hard by, Madame Veuve

Dusuel and Madame Danquin, kept piling logs on the fire and drinking mulled wine, while my mother lay on her bed of suffering.

"Groan away, Madame Nozière, groan all you can," said Madame Caumont, "it will ease the pains."

Madame Dusuel, not knowing what to do with her daughter Alphonsine, aged seven, had brought her into the room, from which, however, she kept hastily thrusting her lest I should dawn, with unbecoming abruptness, on the view of this very young lady; for that would have been a most unseemly occurrence.

These ladies had well-oiled tongues, it seemed, and cackled away quite in the good old fashion. Madame Caumont, to my mother's great displeasure, kept telling the most horrible tales of the sinister effects of the "Evil Eye." She had a friend who, when she was in an interesting condition, met a legless woman holding a laundry iron in each hand and begging alms of the passers-by. That friend's child was born without legs. She herself, when she was expecting her daughter Noémi, was frightened by a hare which rushed in between her legs; and, behold, Noémi was born with pointed ears that waggled!

At midnight the pains ceased and matters were at a standstill. It was an anxious time, particularly as my mother had previously had a still-born

child and nearly lost her life. All the women insisted on giving advice. Madame Mathias, the old
servant, was at her wits' end. My father came
in every five minutes looking very pale and went
out again without a word. Himself a clever and
capable practitioner—physician, surgeon and, when
need was, accoucheur—he would not attend his own
wife in her confinement and had called in his con-
frère, old Dr. Fournier, who had been a student
under Cabanis. During the night the pains came
on again, and I made my appearance at five o'clock
in the morning.

"It's a boy!" said old Fournier.

Whereupon all the gossips exclaimed with one
accord that they had declared all along that it
would be.

Madame Morin washed me with a big sponge in
a copper basin, a circumstance which recalls the
old paintings of the nativity of the Virgin. In point
of fact the utensil in question was the household
preserving-pan. Madame Morin informed the company that I had a red spot on the left hip due to a
longing for cherries which had come upon my mother
in Aunt Chausson's garden before I was born.
Whereat old Dr. Fournier, who had a great contempt for all such popular superstitions, remarked
that it was lucky Madame Nozière had kept her
desires within such modest limits during the period
of gestation, since, if she had allowed herself to

hanker after feathers, trinkets, a cashmere shawl, a coach-and-four, a town-house, a country mansion and a park, there wouldn't have been skin enough on the whole of my poor little body to hold the record of such inordinate ambitions.

"You may say what you like, Doctor," said Madame Caumont, "but one Christmas Eve, my sister Malvina, who was in the family way, was seized with an irresistible desire to stay up and take part in the revels, and her little girl——"

"Was born with a black pudding at the end of her nose, wasn't she?" interrupted the Doctor. And he told Madame Morin to be careful not to bind me too tightly.

Meanwhile I set up such a yelling that they all thought I was going to choke. I was as red as a tomato and unanimously pronounced an ugly little creature. My mother asked them to let her see me. She raised herself nearly upright in the bed, stretched out her arms, smiled on me and then let her head fall wearily back on the pillow again. Thus it was that, for welcome into this world, I received from her pure and tender lips that smile without which, the poet says, a man is unworthy of the table of the gods or of the couch of the goddesses.

What I have always looked upon as the most notable circumstance about my birth was that Puck, since named Caire, came into the world at the same time as myself, being born in the next room on an old bit of carpet. Finette, his mother, though her parents were nobodies, had plenty of brains. M. Adelestan Bricou, an old friend of my father's, who was a liberal and an ardent reformer, used triumphantly to quote Finette as exemplifying the intelligence of the lower orders. Puck bore no resemblance to his dark and fluffy mother; his coat was tan, close and wiry, but it was from her that he derived his common manners and his uncommon brain. We grew up together and my father was compelled to admit that his dog's intelligence developed more rapidly than his son's, and that, after six years or so, Puck was in much closer touch with life and had a far better knowledge of nature than little Pierre Nozière. It was an unwelcome conclusion for him to come to because he was my father and also because his tenets scarcely permitted him to credit the lower animals with any portion of that superior wisdom which, according to his idea, was the exclusive birthright of man.

Napoleon, in his St. Helena days, expressed surprise that O'Meara, being a doctor, was not also an atheist. Had he seen my father, he would have beheld a man who was at once a doctor and a believer in the unseen and, as such, a believer in a god distinct from the world and in a soul distinct from the body.

"The soul," he used to say, "is the substance; the body, the shadow or appearance. The words themselves tell you that. Appearance is what is visible, and substance means the thing hidden."

Unfortunately I was never able to interest myself in metaphysics. My mind was modelled on my father's, but after the manner of the cup that the craftsman moulded on his mistress's breast It reproduced, in intaglio as it were, all its soft and rounded curves. My father regarded the human soul and its destiny as sublime. He believed it was made for heaven and his belief rendered him an optimist. Yet in the ordinary intercourse of life he was grave and sometimes gloomy. Like Lamartine, he seldom laughed, had no sense of the comic, could not tolerate caricature and cared neither for Rabelais nor La Fontaine. Wrapt in a sort of poetic melancholy, he was indeed a child of the age. He felt and looked the part. The way he did his hair, the clothes he wore, were in harmony with the spirit of those romantic times. The men of that epoch wore their hair tumbled. Doubtless a skilful twist of the brush imparted this *négligé* appearance to their locks; but they looked as though they were perpetually fronting the tempest and braving the blasts of Boreas. My father, plain and unaffected as he was, would nevertheless have his hair in disorder and his touch of melancholy. Taking my cue from him, I became just as pessimistic and merry as he was optimistic and melancholy. Instinctively I went contrary to him in everything. After the manner of the Romanticists, he took pleasure in the vague and shadowy, while I cultivated a love for the stately moderation, the ordered beauty, of classic art. As the years went by, the contrast between us grew more marked. But though it made conversation a little difficult for us, it had no effect upon the warmth of our regard for each other. This, then, explains how it is that I owe to my excellent father my few good points and my many bad ones.

My mother, though her milk was not abundant, was very anxious to nurse me herself. In this she was seconded by old Dr. Fournier, a disciple of Jean-Jacques, and she gave me the breast with a lively joy. My health throve therefrom and I have good reason to bless her if, as many folks say, our disposition depends on the milk we suck.

My mother was endowed with charming intellectual gifts, a beautiful and generous soul and a difficult temper. Too sensitive, too loving, too prone to emotion to find peace within herself, she found, she said, tranquility and contentment in religion. Sparing of outward observances, she was nevertheless profoundly pious in spirit. A strict regard for the truth compels me to add that she did not believe in hell. But her disbelief was founded neither in contumacy nor in malice, since the Abbé Moinier, her confessor, did not refuse her the sacraments. Though she was naturally disposed to gaiety, a joyless childhood, followed by household cares and the anxieties born of a mother's love that almost amounted to a passion, clouded her disposition and, strong as she was by nature, affected her health. She brought sorrow into my childhood by her fits of melancholy and her storms of weeping. Her tenderness, her anxiety for me, were so great as almost to unbalance her reason, which in all other matters was so firm and lucid. She would have liked me never to grow up, so that it might always be easy for her to press me to her bosom. And, though she said she hoped I should be a genius, she rejoiced that I lacked brains and consequently had to rely on her. Anything that seemed to promise me a little freedom or independence gave umbrage to her. She would picture to herself all the terrible things that might befall me away from her side, and if I came back from a walk a little late I would find her with her brain in a whirl and panic staring from her eyes. She praised up my good qualities beyond all reason and never lost an opportunity of holding them up to the admiration of others. This was very painful to me, for I have always looked upon testimonies of regard which I did not deserve as a cruel humiliation. Still worse, however, was the equally exaggerated view that my poor mother took of my faults and shortcomings. She never punished me for them, but she made them the subject of reproaches uttered in such sorrowful tones that they nearly broke my heart. Times without number, the things she said were calculated to make me think I was a great criminal and she would have made me scrupulous to excesss, had I not, early in my career, drawn up for my own use an indulgent rule of conduct. Far from experiencing regret at so doing I have never ceased to pat myself on the back•for it. They alone are gentle to others who are gentle to themselves.

I was christened at the parish church of Saint-Germain-des-Prés. My godmother was a fairy known among mortals as Marcelle. She was lovely as the light of day and had married an imp named Dupont whom she loved to distraction, for fairies adore imps. She weaved a spell over my cradle and sailed away at once to a land beyond the seas in company with her imp. I caught sight of her for one fleeting moment when I was on the verge of manhood. She seemed like the stricken shade of Dido in the grove of myrtle, like a ray of moonlight in a forest clearing. It was but a glimpse, but it left within the chambers of my memory a radiance and a perfume that faint not, nor fade. The recollection I have of my godfather, M. Pierre Danquin, is of a more commonplace description. I can see him now, short and fat, his grey hair all curly, his eyes shining kindly and keen through his gold-rimmed spectacles. His corporation, which would have done credit to Grimod de la Reynière, was adorned with a satin waistcoat whereon flowers had been em-

broidered by Madame Danquin's own hand. He
used to wear a great black silk cravat that went
seven times round his neck and the collar of his
shirt encircled his florid face like a piece of white
paper wrapped round a bunch of flowers. He had
seen Napoleon at Lyons in 1815. For the rest, he
was a liberal in politics and much taken up with
geology.

It was in one of the streets which lead down to
the Seine and its quays that a child was born, who
even now, after all this lapse of years, cannot tell
whether he did well or ill to come into the world.
Here, too, where a nameless multitude of men and
women were living out their dim, inglorious lives,
there dwelt a man with a mighty head, rugged and
gaunt as a block of Breton granite, whose eyes, deep
sunken in their hollow sockets, had once blazed with
a quenchless fire of which there now survived but a
faint and fading glimmer. This old man, morose,
infirm, yet proud of mien, this old man who had been
the glory of his generation, was then slowly and
sorrowfully sinking into the grave. His name was
Chateaubriand.

Sometimes, from the heights of Passy, another
old man used to come down to stroll along these
same quays. He was bald save for a few straggling
grey hairs. His cheeks were full and ruddy, he had
a rose in his buttonhole and a smile on his lips. He
was just as bourgeois in appearance as the other was

aristocratic. He was a popular song writer and the passers-by would stop to take a glimpse of him. Chateaubriand, the Royalist and the Catholic; Bérenger, the admirer of Napoleon, the upholder of the Republic, the free thinker—such were the two *signs* beneath whose influence I came into this world.

CHAPTER II

EARLY DAYS

Y earliest memory is of a tall hat, with very long nap, and a very wide brim. It was lined with green silk and the upper part of its inner band of tan leather was cut into strips bent downwards like the leaves of a closed crown save that, as these strips did not completely join, you could catch a glimpse, through a round opening, of a red bandana poked in betwixt the leather band and the gold stamped crown. A white-haired old gentleman would be shown into the drawing-room, holding this hat in his hands. He would then proceed to draw from it, in my presence, the red silk snuff-stained handkerchief which, when unfolded, exhibited Napoleon in his grey overcoat on the top of the Colonne Vendôme. Then the old gentleman would extract from the depths of the crown a little dry cake which he slowly raised above his head. It was a little flat, round cake, shiny and striped on one side. I used to stretch out my hands to catch hold of it, but the old gentleman would not let it go till he had had his fill of amusement at my

vain efforts and the plaints of my frustrated endeavours. In fine, he played with me as he would
have done with a little dog. And I fancy that, as
soon as I realized this, I resented it, already conscious within me of belonging to that high-mettled
race that tame all animals to their will.

These cakes, when you put your teeth into them,
broke as it were into sand in the mouth, but this
sand was soon reduced to a sort of sugary paste by
no means unpleasant despite the bitter taste of tobacco which, now and again, obtruded itself. I
liked them, or thought I did, until I discovered that
they came from an old bakehouse in the Rue de
Seine where they reposed dejectedly in a dubious
looking jar of greenish glass. I thereupon conceived a disgust for them which I failed sufficiently
to conceal from the old gentleman, who grew sad
thereat. I learned afterwards that the old gentleman's name was Morisson and that he had been a
surgeon-major in the British army in 1815.

One evening after the battle of Waterloo, in the
Officers' Mess, the talk got on the prominent men
who had been killed. As the deaths of various
people were being deplored, M. Morisson broke
in saying:

"There is one death, gentlemen, you have over-
looked, one that is more to be regretted than any,
one that we should lament most bitterly of all."

Every one wanted to know to whose death he alluded.

"Gentlemen," said he, "I refer to the death of Promotion. Our victory, by terminating Bonaparte's career, has put an end to the wars which brought us rapid advancement. Promotion was killed at Waterloo; let us mourn its passing, gentlemen."

M. Morisson resigned his commission and came and settled down in Paris, where he married and set up in practice. There he and his wife were both carried off by cholera in 1848.

It was also about this time that, coming into the drawing-room one day holding on to Madame Mathias's apron, I saw a dark man there with big whiskers (it was M. Debas, surnamed Simon de Nantua) repairing, with a paint brush soaked in glue, the green striped wall-paper, about a foot of which was torn and hanging down. The rent disclosed a piece of coarse canvas with a great hole in it, and, behind the canvas, a darksome cavity. These things impressed themselves upon me with great vividness, and they still remain strangely distinct in my memory though so many other sights presented to my vision in those far-off days have utterly faded from my recollection. Doubtless I did not think much about the matter at the time, not having arrived at the reflective age. But some time afterwards, when I was nearing my fourth year, and

had sufficient brains to reason erroneously and sufficient education to misinterpret phenomena, I conceived the notion that, behind this coarse canvas
with its covering of striped paper, unknown beings
were hovering in the darkness, beings that were different from men or birds or fishes or insects; vague,
shadowing things yet cunning withal and full of evil
intent. Thus it was not without curiosity, not without terror, that I used to pass by the place where M.
Debas had repaired the rent in the paper, a rent
that still remained visible, since the edges of the
green paper had not been so thoroughly joined but
that you could just catch between them a glimpse
of a piece of newspaper that had been stuck on as
a foundation; not perhaps æsthetic, but comforting,
since it deprived those spirits of darkness, those
dim sinister creatures of two dimensions, of the
power of access to the room.

Once upon a time (as Eastern story-tellers say,
being, like myself, doubtful in their chronology) one
fine day in my fourth year, I noticed near the piano
another hole, shaped like a star, in the green wall-
paper, through which you could see a few threads
of packing-cloth interlaced across a black hole even
more fearsome than the one previously stopped up
by M. Debas. With an impious daring, worthy of
the bold race of Japhet, I put my eye close to the
opening and there beheld living shadows that made
my hair stand on end. I then applied my ear to the

spot and heard an uncanny murmur, what time an
icy breath passed along my cheek, all of which con-
firmed me in the belief that, behind the wall-paper,
there existed another and an unknown world.

My life, at this period, was a double one. Natural, commonplace, occasionally even wearisome, by
day, it became supernatural and terrible at night.
Round about my little bed, wherein my mother used
to tuck me up with her own fair hands, there used
to pass by, in a wild, fantastic rout, yet not without
rhythm and measure, a procession of little mis-
shapen, hump-backed, crooked personages clad in
very antique fashion, such, in fine, as I have since
discovered in Callot's engravings. Certainly I had
never invented them. The fact that Madame Letord dwelt hard by, Madame Letord a print-seller
who displayed her engravings on the piece of waste
land now occupied by the École des Beaux-Arts, explains the circumstance. Howbeit my imagination
played its part too. It armed my nocturnal perse-
cutors with spigots and squirts, and little brooms and
divers other household utensils. This, however, did
not detract from the gravity with which they filed
past, their noses blossoming with warts and bestrid
with round barnacles. Yet they were in a great
hurry, withal, and appeared not to notice me.

One evening, while the lamp was still burning, my
father came and stood by my little bed and gazed at
me with the exquisite smile of sad hearted men with

whom smiles are rare. I was already half asleep as he quietly caressed the palm of my hand humming a little nursery rhyme of which I caught nothing save the words, "I've got a cow to sell." And I, not seeing any cow, inquired, sensibly enough, "Papa, where is the cow you've got to sell?"

I fell asleep and saw my father again in my dream. This time, he was holding a little red and white cow in the hollow of his hand. It was quite lively and spirited, so much alive that its breath was warm to me and it smelt of the cow-shed. For many nights afterwards I saw that little red and white cow.

CHAPTER III

ALPHONSINE

LPHONSINE DUSUEL was seven years older than I, and a thin, weedy creature. She had greasy hair and a freckled face. Unless I am very far wrong these characteristics afterwards constituted her most inexcusable defects in the eyes of the world. I knew that she had others not so serious, such as hypocrisy and spite, which were so much a part of her nature that they almost became her.

One day my dear mother was taking me for a walk on the quay when we met Madame Dusuel and her daughter. We stopped, and the two ladies had a little talk together.

"Oh, the pet, how pretty he is!" exclaimed Alphonsine, flinging her arms round me.

Though at that time I had not as much intelligence as a dog or a cat, I was, like them, a domestic animal and, like them, I loved those words of praise which creatures in their wild state despise. In an access of affection which touched the two mothers' hearts, dear Alphonsine picked me up, pressed me to her heart and smothered me with kisses, saying all the while what a darling little fellow I was. At the same time she was busily pricking my legs with a pin. And so I began to fight like fury, punching and kicking Alphonsine, yelling and shedding floods of tears.

Beholding this, Madame Dusuel betrayed, by her silence and the expression in her eyes, the surprise and indignation she felt at such conduct. My mother gazed at me in sorrow and marvelled how she could have brought so unnatural a child into the world, now blaming heaven for visiting her with unmerited misfortune, now finding fault with herself for having incurred it by her own shortcomings. At last she stood silent and perplexed before the insoluble mystery of my perversity. How was I to explain it to her, however, if I could not talk? The few words which I was able to babble were of no service to me in the present crisis. Planted at length on my feet, I stood there panting and tearful. And Alphonsine, bending over me, wiped my eyes, petted me, and pleaded for me:

"He is such a tiny little fellow. Please don't scold him, Madame Nozière. I should be so sorry; I am so fond of him."

Not once only, but a score of times did Alphonsine embrace me ecstatically and dig pins into my legs.

Later on, when I could talk, I denounced her perfidy to my mother and to Madame Mathias, who had the care of me. But they didn't believe me.

They blamed me for slandering the innocent in order to palliate my own misdeeds.

It is a long time ago, now, since I forgave Alphonsine her cruel deceit, and even her greasy hair. Nay more, I am grateful to her for having vastly added, when I was but two years old, to my knowledge of human nature.

CHAPTER IV

O long as I was unable to read, newspapers had a mysterious attraction for me. When I used to see my father spreading out their big sheets covered all over with little black signs, when passages were read aloud and connected ideas were produced from those same signs, it seemed to me as though I were a party to some work of magic. From this sheet so thin and covered with lines so tiny, lines that had no signification in my eyes, there issued tidings of crimes, disasters, adventures, festivals—of Napoleon Bonaparte escaping from the fort of Ham; of Tom Thumb dressed up like a general; of the stalled Ox Dagobert being led through Paris; of the murder of the Duchesse de Praslin. All these things were contained in a single sheet of paper, all these things and numberless others besides, things not so solemn but more homely, whereby my curiosity was aroused. There were "Misters" who gave blows or received them, who got run over by vehicles, who fell off roofs or picked up purses and took them to the

police. How came it that there were all these "Misters" about when I never set eyes on a single one? I tried, but in vain, to imagine what a "Mister" was like. I asked people about it, but never got any satisfactory answer.

In those far distant times Madame Mathias used to come to our house to help Mélanie, with whom she didn't get on at all well. Madame Mathias was grim, hot-tempered and easily ruffled, but she took a lot of interest in me. She invented all sorts of subtle devices to make a better boy of me. She pretended, for example, to discover in the newspaper, under "Paris Day by Day," sandwiched in between an "alleged case of arson," and an accident to "Mr. Duchesne, labourer," an account of my conduct on the previous day. "Yesterday," she would read, "little Pierre Nozière was naughty and would not do as he was told in the Jardin des Tuileries; but he has promised not to behave badly any more."

I was wide enough awake, when I was two years old, to feel a certain difficulty in believing that I was mentioned in the newspapers, like M. Guizot and Mr. Duchesne, labourer. I noticed that Madame Mathias, who could read the news of the day, a little stumblingly perhaps, but without having to correct herself over much, used to stammer in the most singular manner when she came to the items which had to do with me. I therefore arrived at the conclusion that they were not printed in the paper at all, but that she used to make them up as she went along, without being quite equal to the task. In short, I was not wholly taken in, yet it was not without a pang that I renounced the glory of figuring in print and I preferred in my heart to regard the matter as doubtful rather than to possess the certainty that it was false.

CHAPTER V

WHAT CAME OF AN ERROR OF JUDGMENT

ERE is another memory gathered up amid the twilight of those far-off days. A little thing, perhaps, but then origins always have for us the fascination of mystery and, as we cannot trace the well-springs of human thought, it is at all events interesting to note the signs of the dawning of intelligence in a child. And, if there is nothing singular or exceptional about the child, it is all the more valuable as an object of study, inasmuch as it represents in itself a host of other children. That is one reason why I am going to relate my anecdote. Another is that I shall be pleasing myself mightily in the process.

One day—I cannot express myself with greater precision than that, for the place of that day in the order of time is lost beyond recall—one day, I say, I had been for a walk with Mélanie, my old nurse, and when I got home, I went, as usual, to my mother's room. There I noticed an odour that I could not identify and that came, as I afterwards discovered, from a smoky chimney. It was not pungent or choking, but faint, pervasive and sickly. Nevertheless it didn't annoy me much for, as regards the olfactory sense, I was, in those days, more akin to the little dog Caire than to M. Robert de Montesquiou, the poet of perfumes. Now it chanced that, while this unknown, or rather unidentified, odour was titillating my inexperienced nostrils, my dear mother put into my hand a sort of emerald coloured stick, about as long as a dessert knife, but ever so much thicker. It seemed to me a marvellous delicacy invested with all the charm of the unknown. I had never before seen anything to come near it.

"Taste it," said my mother, "it's very nice."

And it was. When you bit it, the stem split up into little sugary splinters that had a flavour that was undeniably pleasant and more delicate than any of the sweets and sugar-stuffs I had tasted up to then.

The sweetness of this plant was such that I fell a-dreaming of the fruits of that land where rivers of gooseberry syrup flow through rocks of caramel, though truth to tell my belief in the Land of Cocagne was no greater than Virgil's in those Elysian Fields belauded of the Greeks:

"Quamvis elysios miretur Græcia campos"

but, like Virgil, I loved tales of enchantment, and my mind was filled with wonder, for I did not know, in those days, what the confectioners do to a stalk

of angelica to render it so pleasant to the palate.
For this highly delectable rod was nothing else than
a piece of angelica given to my dear mother by Madame Caumont, who had had a whole boxful sent her
from Niort.

Coming in a few days later from my usual walk
with Mélanie, my nurse, I noticed in my mother's
room the same peculiar sickly smell which I had
perceived when I saw angelica for the first time and
which I therefore took to be the smell of angelica.

I kissed my mother with ceremonious punctilio.
She asked me if I had enjoyed my walk, and I said
I had; if I had worried Mélanie too much, and I
said I hadn't. Having thus performed my duties as
a son, I waited for my mother to give me a piece
of angelica. As, however, she had taken up her
needle-work again and gave no sign of performing
the pleasing act for which I was waiting, I decided
to make a request for my piece of angelica, which
I did, though not without reluctance, so great was
the delicacy of my sentiments. Mamma looked up
from her work, with an air of some surprise and
said she hadn't any.

Unwilling to suspect her of telling a lie, however
trifling a one, I told myself she was joking and
that she was putting off the appeasement of my longing, either because she wanted to render it the
greater or because she was indulging in the bad

habit grown-up people have of deriving amusement from the impatience of dogs and children.

I urged her to give me my piece of angelica. She replied, a second time, that she had no angelica and clearly she intended her reply to be final. Relying, alas, on the testimony of my senses and on the verdict of my reasoning faculty, I answered with assurance that there was angelica somewhere in the room because I could smell it.

The history of Science abounds in examples of similar faulty deductions, and the world's greatest geniuses have often been misled in the same manner as little Pierre Nozière. That little person ascribed to one substance a certain property that belonged to another. In physics and chemistry there are laws reposing on foundations just as false, laws that are respected and will go on being respected till time at last brings about their abrogation.

These reflections did not suggest themselves to my mother's mind. She merely shrugged her shoulders and told me I was a little silly. That was too much for me. I told her I was not a little silly, that there *was* angelica there because I could smell it and that it was not seemly for a mamma to tell falsehoods to her little boy. On hearing this reproach, my mother gazed at me with an expression of profound and sorrowful surprise. I was suddenly convinced, when I saw this look in her eyes, that my dear mamma had not deceived me and that, despite the evidence of my senses, there was no angelica in the house.

And so, on that occasion, my heart came to the rescue of my reason. I would fain draw the conclusion that we should always regulate our actions according to the dictates of our heart. That would be the moral of the story and all affectionate souls would welcome it. But the truth must be told, even if it causes disappointment. The heart can err as well as the intellect; its errors are no less ruinous and it is more difficult to escape from them, by reason of the honey that besmears their meshes.

CHAPTER VI

THE FATE OF GENIUS

ENIUS is fated to meet with injustice and contempt, a truth whereof I early made probation. When I was four, I used to be an ardent draughtsman. Nevertheless I did not essay to depict all the objects that presented themselves to my view; it only portrayed soldiers. If the truth must be told, I did not draw them according to nature. Nature is complex and does not lend herself to easy imitation. Nor did I draw them according to the coloured prints which they produce at Épinal and which I used to buy at a halfpenny apiece. These likewise exhibited a super-abundance of detail through which I should never have found my way. I decided to take as my model the simplified recollection of those same prints. My soldiers had a round "O" for a head, a line for the body and a line for each arm and leg. A line with a crook in it, like a streak of lightning, represented the rifle with bayonet fixed, and it was eminently expressive. I did not fit the shako down on to the head. I placed it just on the top in order to demonstrate my scientific knowl-

edge of the subject and to display at once the shape of the head and that of the headgear. I drew a large number after this style, a style common to all children's drawings. They were skeletons, if you will, and very sketchy ones at that. But, such as they were, I deemed my soldiers very passably well executed. I drew them in pencil, copiously wetting the point to make it mark the better. I would rather have used a pen, but ink was not allowed me for fear I should make a mess. Nevertheless I was pleased with my handiwork and considered myself a person of talent. I was destined in no long time to astonish even myself.

One evening, one memorable evening, I was busy drawing on the dining-room table which Mélanie had just cleared. The lamp, with its green shade like a Chinaman's hat, shed a warm glow upon my paper. I had already drawn five or six soldiers after my customary method, which I practised with facility, when, all of a sudden, I was visited with a flash of genius. I conceived the idea of representing arms and legs not by a single line but by two parallel lines. I thus achieved a result that conveyed a striking semblance of reality. It was the living thing. I gazed at it in delight. Dædalus, when he created his walking statues, was not more pleased with his handiwork than I. True, I might have asked myself whether I was the first to think of so pleasing a device and whether I had

not already seen examples of it. I asked myself no
such questions; I asked myself no questions at
all, but, with staring eyes and protruding tongue,
I sat gazing like one dazed at what I had done.
And then, since it is the nature of artists to hold
up their works to the admiration of mankind, I went
over to my mother who was reading a book, and
extending my scrawl before her eyes, exclaimed:

"Look!"

Seeing that she was paying no attention to what
I was showing her, I laid my soldiers on the page
that she was reading.

She was patience itself.

"It's very nice," she said gently, but in a voice
which showed she did not adequately appreciate the
revolution I had just effected in the art of drawing.

"Mamma, look!" I repeated again and again.

"Yes, I see, very nice, now run away."

"No, you don't see, mamma," I said, endeavouring to snatch away the book that was diverting her
attention from my masterpiece.

She forbade me to touch the book with my dirty
hands.

"But you're not looking!" I cried in desperation.

She would not deign to take any further notice,
and ordered me to be quiet.

Exasperated by an attitude so blind and so unjust, I stamped my feet, burst out crying and tore
my masterpiece to shreds.

"How excitable the child is," said my mother with a sigh as she led me away to bed.

I was a prey to dark despair. For just imagine! After having given an immense impetus to the arts, after creating a prodigiously effective means of portraying life, all I got in the way of recompense and glory was—to be sent to bed!

Shortly after this reverse, I suffered another one that inflicted a wound no less cruel. It befell thus: my mother had taught me pretty soon to form my letters with tolerable skill. Being able to write a little, I thought there was nothing to prevent my composing a book and so, beneath the eye of my dear mamma, I set my hand to a little moral and theological treatise which I began thus, "What is God . . ." and forthwith I took it to my mother to ask her if that was right. My mother replied that it was quite right except that a note of interrogation was needed at the end of the sentence. I asked her what a note of interrogation was.

"A note of interrogation," said my mother, "is a sign used to signify that one is asking a question. It is placed at the end of every interrogative sentence. You should put a note of interrogation here because you ask, "What is God?"

My answer was noble.

"I am not asking," I said proudly, "I know."

"But you are asking, dear," she replied.

A score of times I repeated that I was not asking because I knew, and, I flatly refused to add that note of interrogation which seemed to me to be merely a mark of ignorance.

My mother upbraided me severely for my obstinacy and said I was nothing more nor less than a silly little boy. Thereat my *amour-propre* as a writer was wounded and I replied with some impertinent remark for which I was duly punished.

I have changed a great deal since then. I never refuse now to put notes of interrogation in the places where it is customary to employ them. I am sorely tempted indeed to add very big ones after everything I write, or say, or think. Perhaps, were she living now, my poor mother would say I use too many.

CHAPTER VII

NAVARINO

S far back as I could remember I had known Madame Laroque, who, with her daughter, occupied a little flat at the other end of our courtyard. She was a little old lady from Normandy, the widow of a Captain in the Imperial Guards. All her teeth had gone and her soft lips were tightly drawn in over her gums; but her cheeks were round and ruddy as the apples of her native country. Having no idea of the instability of Nature and the transience of material things, I regarded her as coeval with the earliest period of the world and endowed with an imperishable old age. From my mother's room you could see Madame Laroque's window festooned with nasturtiums, and on the sill of it her parrot swung to and fro on its perch, trolling forth snatches of ribald songs and patriotic ballads. He had been brought from the East Indies in 1827 and had been christened Navarino, in memory of the naval victory gained by the combined fleets of France and England over the Turks, the news of which reached Paris on the day of his arrival. Madame Laroque

petted him like a baby, and put him in the window
every morning in order that the old fellow might
enjoy the bustle and animation of the courtyard.
Of a truth, I cannot make out what sort of pleasure the old Yankee derived from looking at Au-
guste washing M. Bellaguet's carriage or the aged
Alexandre pulling up the grass that grew between
the paving stones; but in point of fact he seemed
scarcely at all dispirited from his long exile. Without claiming to read what things were in his mind,
one might have supposed that he was delighting in
his strength, and he was indeed an animal of singular toughness. When his little grey claws closed
round a piece of wood, he would tear it to shreds
with his beak in less than no time.

I have always been fond of animals; but in
those days they inspired me with veneration and a
sort of religious fear. I had a notion that they were
possessed of a more unerring intelligence than my
own and a deeper understanding of Nature. The
poodle, Zerbin, always seemed to me to compre-
hend things that were beyond my ken and our beautiful Angora, Sultan Mahmud, who understood the
language of birds, I used to look upon as a mysterious spirit endowed with the power of reading
the future. My mother one day took me to the
Louvre, where, in the Egyptian galleries, I saw the
mummies of domestic animals swathed in bandages
and covered with aromatics. "The Egyptians," she

told me, "adored them as divinities and, when they died, carefully embalmed them."

I do not know what ideas the ancient Egyptians entertained concerning the ibis and the cat; I do not know whether, as some people hold nowadays, animals were the first gods worshipped by men; but I came very near to ascribing supernatural powers to Sultan Mahmud and to Zerbin, the poodle. That which rendered them most marvellous in my eyes was that they appeared to me in my sleep and held converse with me. One night, in a dream, I beheld Zerbin scratch away at the ground and presently unearth a hyacinth bulb.

"This," he said, "is what little children are like in the Earth before they are born; they unfold like flowers."

So, you see, I loved animals. I admired their wisdom and plied them with questions somewhat anxiously during the day so that they should come to me by night and instruct me in natural philosophy. Birds were by no means excluded from my friendship and from my veneration. I would have cherished Navarino with filial affection; I would have bestowed unnumbered tokens of solicitude and regard on this aged Cacique; I would have become his docile disciple, if only he would have let me. But he would not suffer me so much as to look at him. Whenever I drew near he would swing impatiently on his perch, ruffle up the feathers on his

neck, stare me full in the face with eyes of fire,
open his beak menacingly and display a black tongue
as thick as a haricot bean. I should have liked to
know the cause of his unfriendliness. Madame Laroque ascribed it to the circumstance that, when
I was quite little, and before I was able to walk,
I used to insist on being carried up to his perch,
stretched out my baby fingers to touch his eyes that
blazed like rubies and howled shrilly because I could
not reach them. She loved her parrot and tried
to make excuses for him. But who would have
credited the existence of so rooted and tenacious a
resentment?

Well, whatever its cause, Navarino's hostility
seemed to me both cruel and unjust. Anxious to
regain the good graces of this puissant yet fearsome being, I deemed that gifts might appease him
and that an offering of sugar might prove accept-
able in his eyes. In contravention of my mother's
express injunctions, I opened the cupboard of the
side-board in the dining-room and selected the finest
and most attractive looking knob in the sugar-basin;
for it must here be observed that, in those days,
sugar was not broken up by machinery as it is now.
Housekeepers used to buy it in the loaf and, in
our family, the aged Mélanie, armed with a ham-
mer and an old broken knife minus its handle, used
to break it up into pieces of various shapes and
sizes, scattering an abundance of splinters in the

process, after the manner of a geologist chipping off samples of ore from the solid rock. Nor must I omit to add that sugar was very dear then. With my heart filled with peace and goodwill, my offering safely stowed in the pocket of my pinafore, I proceeded to Madame Laroque's apartment and found Navarino at his window. He was cracking grains of hemp-seed with an air of leisurely nonchalance. Deeming the moment opportune, I held out the lump of sugar to the aged chieftain. He did accept the proffered gift. He looked at me for a long time sideways, in silent immobility; then suddenly swooped down on my finger and bit at it. The blood began to flow.

Madame Laroque has often told me that, as soon as I beheld the colour of my blood, I uttered the most terrific shrieks, wept copiously and asked if I should die. I have always been loath to accept her version of the story. All the same, it is possible that there may have been some modicum of truth in it. She comforted me and tied a rag round my finger.

I went home indignant, my bosom bursting with hatred and fury. Between Navarino and me it was war from that day forth; war, stern and pitiless. Whenever we met I proceeded to insult and provoke him, and he would fly into a rage; that, to do him justice, was a satisfaction of which he never deprived me. Sometimes I tickled his neck with a straw, sometimes I pelted him with bread pills and he would open his beak wide and in hoarse tones rasp out all manner of unintelligible threats. Madame Laroque, knitting as her custom was, a width of a flannel petticoat, used to look at me over her spectacles.

"Pierre," she would say, threatening me with her wooden needle, "let that creature alone. You know what he did to you before. Mark my words, something worse will happen next time, if you don't leave off."

I disregarded this sage warning, and I had reason to regret it. One day, when I was playing havoc with his feeding tray, throwing about his maize seed, the old warrior leapt upon me, and plunging his claws into my hair, mauled and tore at my head with his talons. If the infant Ganymede was scared by the ravishing eagle that gathered him lovingly in his soft embrace, judge of the terror I felt when Navarino began tearing at my head with his iron claws. My yells were heard right down on the banks of the Seine. Madame Laroque, laying down her everlasting knitting, detached the American from his prey and bore him back on her shoulder to his perch. Thence, his neck ruffled with arrogance, the spoils of my hair tangled in his claws, he glared at me in triumph with a fiery eye. My overthrow was complete, my humiliation profound.

A few days later, I made my way into our kitchen,

where countless delights exerted an unceasing fascination over me; and there I saw the aged Mélanie chopping up parsley on a board with a knife. I put several questions to her regarding this herb, whose pungent odour titillated my nostrils. Mélanie favoured me with copious information concerning it. She imparted to me that parsley was used in stews and as a seasoning for grilled meats. Finally she told me that it was a deadly poison for parrots. On hearing this, I snatched up a sprig which had escaped the knife and took it into the rose-papered cabinet, where I meditated alone and in silence. I held the doom of Navarino in my hands. After deliberating long within me, I quitted the apartment and betook myself to Madame Laroque's; there I displayed to Navarino the death-dealing herb.

"Look here," I said to him, "this is parsley! If I were to mix up these little green, curly leaves with your hemp-seed you would die and I should have my revenge. But I intend to reap another sort of vengeance. I am going to revenge myself by letting you live," and with these words I flung the fatal herb out of the window.

From that day forth I ceased to worry Navarino. I made up my mind that nothing should mar my clemency. We became friends.

CHAPTER VIII

HOW IT EARLY BECAME EVIDENT THAT I LACKED THE BUSINESS SENSE

T was before the Revolution of '48; I was not yet four, that is certain, but was I three and a half? That is what I cannot be quite sure of, and now, for this many a year there has been no one left on earth who could throw any light on the point. One must make the best of this uncertainty, and console oneself with the reflection that more important and more exasperating lacunæ present themselves in the history of nations. Chronology and geography, it has been said, are the two eyes of history. If that be so, everything leads one to conclude that, despite the Benedictines of Saint-Maur, who invented the art of verifying dates, History is, to say the least of it, blind of one eye. And, let me add, that is the least of its defects. Clio, the muse Clio, is a personage of grave and occasionally somewhat austere deportment, and her erudite discourse, as we are told, is calculated to interest, to inspire and to amuse; one could listen to her readily a whole day long. Yet have I noticed, from long and assiduous cultivation of her company,

49

that she but too often allows it to be seen that she is forgetful, vain, biased, ignorant and untruthful. Yet with all her faults I have loved her much and love her still. These are the only bonds that unite me to Clio. She has nothing to record of my childhood nor, for that matter, of the rest of my life. Happily, I am by no means an historic personage and proud Clio will never seek to discover whether I was at the beginning, the middle or the end of my third year when I betrayed an indication of character that deeply impressed my mother.

I was then a very ordinary child, with, if I remember rightly, nothing original in my composition, save a certain reluctance to swallow everything that people told me. This characteristic, the mark of an inquiring mind, used to get me into bad odour, for it is not the critical sense that people usually admire in a child of three or three and a half.

I might dispense, if I liked, with making these remarks, for they have just as little to do with the story I am about to relate as chronology, the art of verifying dates and the muse Clio. If I make so many digressions, if I wander away along so many by-paths, I shall never reach my journey's end. But then if I don't amuse myself as I go along, if I keep strictly to the road, I shall get there all at once; I shall have finished in the twinkling of an eye. And that would be a pity, at least for me; for I love to linger by the way. I know nothing more pleasant and at the same time more profitable. Of all the schools I ever went to, Dr. Truant's was the one in which I got on best and learned the most. There is nothing like straying from the beaten track, my friends. If Little Red Riding Hood had gone through the wood without lingering to gather nuts, the wolf wouldn't have eaten her; and every moral person will agree that the best thing that could happen to Little Red Riding Hood and her like is to be eaten up by the wolf.

This reflection brings us conveniently back to the subject of my narrative. I was about to inform you that in the third year of my age and in the eighteenth and last of the reign of Louis Philippe the First, King of France, my greatest pleasure in life was going for walks. They did not send me into the wood, like Little Red Riding Hood; alas, I was not so Arcadian! Born and brought up in the heart of Paris, on the brave Quai Malaquais, I knew not the pleasures of field and hedgerow. But assuredly the town also has its charm. Taking my hand in hers, my mother led me along the streets with their countless sounds, crowded with shifting colours and enlivened by the throng of passers-by; and when she had any purchases to make, she would take me with her into the shops. We were not rich, and she did not spend much money, but the shops she used to visit seemed to me to be unsurpassable in extent and splendour. The Bon Marché, the Louvre, the Printemps, the

Galeries did not exist in those days. The largest establishments, in the latter years of the constitutional monarchy, could only boast a local clientele. My mother, who belonged to the Faubourg Saint-Germain, used to go to the Deux-Magots and the Petit Saint-Thomas.

Of these two shops, one of which was in the Rue de Seine and the other in the Rue du Bac only the latter now survives, but it has grown so big and so different, with the lions' heads that lend terror to its front, from what it was in its early days, that I no longer recognize it. The Deux-Magots have disappeared and perhaps I am the only one left in the world who can recall the big oil painting which served as a shop sign and which represented a young Chinese woman between two of her fellow country men. I was already keenly alive to feminine beauty, and this young Chinese woman, with her hair held back with a large comb and her kiss-curls about her temples, quite took my fancy. But of her two admirers, of their bearing, their expression, their features, their intentions, of these I could say nothing. I knew nothing of the art of captivation.

The shop seemed to me immense and filled with treasures. It was there, perhaps, that I acquired that predilection for sumptuous things which became very strong in me and has never left me since. The sight of the stuffs, the carpets, the embroideries, the feathers, the flowers, threw me into a kind of ecstasy and,

with my whole soul, I used to admire those affable
gentlemen and gracious young ladies who smilingly
offered these marvels to hesitating customers. When
an assistant who was serving my mother measured
out some cloth by means of a yard wand fixed hori-
zontally to a copper rod dependent from the ceiling,
it seemed to me that his calling was splendid and his
destiny glorious.

I also admired M. Augris, the tailor of the Rue
du Bac, who used to fit me with jacket and knickerbockers. I would have preferred him to make me
long trousers and a frock-coat such as the gentlemen
wore; and this desire became very ardent a little
later on when I read a story by Bouilly concerning an
unfortunate little boy who was taken care of by a
worthy and kind-hearted professor. The professor
employed him as his secretary and dressed him in
his old clothes. The worthy Bouilly's story led me
to do a very silly thing, which I will relate another
time. Full of respect for the arts and crafts, I admired M. Augris, the tailor of the Rue du Bac, who
did not merit admiration because he cut his cloth all
awry. Truth to tell, in the clothes he made for me,
I looked like a monkey.

My dear mamma, like the good housekeeper she
was, did her shopping herself, buying her groceries
at Courcelles' in the Rue Bonaparte, her coffee at
Corcelet's in the Palais Royal, and her chocolate
at Debeauve and Gallais' in the Rue des Saints-

Pères. Whether it was that he gave one plenty of sugar-plums to taste, or that he made the crystals of his sugar-loaves glisten in the sun, or that, with a gesture combining boldness and elegance he turned a pot of gooseberry jelly upside down to show how well it had set, M. Courcelles charmed me with his persuasive graces and his convincing demonstrations. I used to get almost angry with my mother because of the doubtful and incredulous air with which she listened to the assurance, always backed with examples, offered by this eloquent grocer. I have since learned that her scepticism was justified.

I can still see Corcelet's shop, at the sign of the "Gourmand"; a little low-ceiled place with the name painted in gilt letters on a red ground. It exhaled a delicious smell of coffee, and there was to be seen there a painting, an old one even in those days, representing a gourmand dressed in the same style as my grandfather. He was seated at a table set out with bottles and a pasty of monstrous size, and adorned with a pineapple by way of decoration. I am in a position to state, thanks to information that came to me a very long time afterwards, that it was a portrait of Grimod de la Reynière by Bouilly. It was with feelings of respect that I used to enter this house, which seemed to belong to another age and to take one back to the Directoire. Corcelet's man weighed and served in silence. The simplicity of his demeanour, which contrasted with the emphatic mannerisms of M. Courcelles, made an impression on me and it may be that my first lessons in taste and moderation were derived by me from an old grocer's assistant.

I never came out of Corcelet's shop without taking a coffee bean to chew on the way. I told myself it was very good and I half believed it was so. I felt in my heart that it was execrable, but I was not yet capable of bringing to light the truths that lay hidden within me. Much as I liked Corcelet's shop, at the sign of the "Gourmand", that of Debeauve and Gallais, purveyors by appointment to the Kings of France, pleased me more and charmed me more than any other. So beautiful did it seem to me, that I did not judge myself worthy of entering therein save in my Sunday clothes, and, on reaching the threshold, I looked carefully at my mother's attire in order to satisfy myself that it was suitably elegant. Well, well, my taste was not so bad! The house of Debeauve and Gallais, chocolate makers to the Kings of France, is still in existence and its appearance has changed but little. I can therefore speak of it from actual knowledge and not from fallacious recollection. It creates a very good impression. Its scheme of decoration dates from the early years of the Restoration, before style in such matters had become too heavy, and it is in the manner of Percier and Fontaine. I cannot help sadly reflecting when I look at these *motifs*, rather frigid, it may be, but delicate, pure and well ordered, how taste in France has deteriorated during the last century. What a distance we have travelled from the decorative art of the Empire, inferior as that was to the style of Louis XVI and the Directoire. In this old-world shop one cannot but admire the sign with its well proportioned, bold lettering; the arched windows with their fan-shaped mouldings the far end of the shop rounded like a little temple, the counter semi-circular in shape following the curve of the room. I don't know whether I am dreaming, but it seems to me that I have seen pier-glasses there adorned with allegorical figures of Fame which might do honour to Arcole and Lodi quite as appropriately as to chocolate creams and chocolate almonds. In fine, the whole thing was consistent. It possessed a character and conveyed a meaning. What do they do nowadays? There are still artists of genius, but the decorative arts have fallen into a most ignominious decline. The style of the Third Republic makes one sigh for Napoleon III; Napoleon III for Louis Philippe; Louis Philippe for Charles X; Charles X for the Directoire; the Directoire for Louis XVI. The sense of line and proportion is completely lost. Therefore I hail with delight the advent of the New Art, not so much, indeed, for what it brings as for what it takes away.

Need I remark that when I was but three or four years old I was not given to discussing the theory of decoration? But, whenever I went into the establishment of Messrs. Debeauve and Gallais, it seemed to me as though I were entering a fairy palace. What assisted the illusion was the sight of certain young ladies there in black gowns, with lustrous hair, seated round the semi-circular counter in attitudes of gracious solemnity. In the midst of them, gentle and grave of mien, sat a lady of riper years, who made entries in registers which reposed on a big desk, and handled pieces of money and bank-notes. It will soon be shown that I quite failed to acquire any adequate understanding of the operations performed by this venerable dame. On either side of her, young ladies, both dark and fair, were busily engaged, some in covering the cakes of chocolate with a thin metal leaf of silvery brightness, others in enveloping these same cakes, two at a time, in white paper wrappers with pictures on them and then sealing these wrappers with wax which they heated in the flame of a little tin lamp. They accomplished these tasks with skill and with a celerity that seemed to betoken delight. I imagine, when I come to think of it now, that they did not work like that for the fun of the thing; but in those days I might quite well have made a mistake, seeing how ready I was to look on any kind of work as a diversion. This at least is certain, that it was a joy to the eye to watch the deft fingers of those young women.

When my mother had completed her purchases, the matron who presided over this assembly of wise virgins extracted from a crystal bowl that stood beside her a chocolate drop, which she offered me with a watery smile. And this solemn gift, more than anything else, made me love and admire the establishment of Messrs. Debeauve and Gallais, purveyors to the Kings of France.

Being fond of all that had to do with shops, it was quite natural that, when I got home, I should try to imitate in my games the scenes I had witnessed while my mother was making her purchases. Thus it came about that, in my father's house, I became all to myself, and without anybody being aware of it, successively a tailor, a grocer, a fancy-goods man and, no less readily, a dressmaker and a chocolate saleswoman. Now it befell that one evening, in the little room with the rosebud wall-paper, where my mother was sitting with her needlework in her hand, I was applying myself with more assiduity than usual to the task of imitating the fair ladies of Messrs. Debeauve and Gallais' establishment. Having collected as many pieces of chocolate as I could lay hands on, together with some bits of paper and even some fragmentary pieces of those metallic leaves which I termed emphatically silver paper, all if the truth be told considerably the worse for wear, I seated myself in my little chair, a present from my Aunt Chausson, with a moleskin stool in front

of me. All of this paraphernalia represented in my
eyes the elegant semi-circle of the store in the Rue
des Saints-Pères. Being an only child, accustomed to
amuse myself and always deep in some day-dream,
passing, that is to say, a great part of my time in
the world of shadows, it was easy enough for me
to summon up to my imagination the absent shop
with its panelling, its glass cabinets, its pier-glasses
adorned with the allegorical figure of Fame and
even the purchasers flocking thither in crowds—
women, children and old men—so great was my
power to evoke at will both scenes and actors. I had
no difficulty in enacting, in my sole person, the young
lady customers, the young demoiselles of the counter
and the highly respectable dame who kept the books
and looked after the cash. My magic power knew
no limits and exceeded all that I have since read
of in *The Golden Ass* concerning the witches of
Thessaly. I could change my nature at will. I was
capable of assuming the strangest and most extraordinary shapes, of becoming, by magic, a King,
a dragon, a demon, a fairy, nay, of changing into
an army, or a river, a forest or a mountain. What
I was attempting that evening was therefore a mere
trifle and offered no difficulty whatever. And so I
wrapped up and I sealed and I served customers
without number—women, children and old men.
Filled with the idea of my own importance (must I
avow it?), I spoke very curtly to my imaginary com-

panions, chiding their slowness and taking them un-
mercifully to task for their mistakes. But, when it
came to playing the part of the aged and respectable
dame who had charge of the cash, I became suddenly
embarrassed. In this crisis I left the shop and went
to ask my dear mamma to clear up a point concerning which I was still in the dark. I had seen the
old dame open her drawer and stir the money about,
but I had never arrived at a sufficiently exact notion
of the nature of the operations performed by her.
Kneeling down at my mother's feet—she was em-
broidering a handkerchief in her deep easy chair—
I asked:

"Mamma, in the shops, is it the people who sell
or the people who buy that pay the money?"

My mother looked at me in wide-eyed surprise,
raised her eyebrows and smiled at me without replying. Then she grew thoughtful. At that moment my father came into the room.

"What do you think Pierrot has just been asking me?" she said. "You will never guess. He
wants to know whether it is the people who buy
or the people who sell that pay the money."

"Oh, the little duffer!" said my father.

"It's not just ordinary childish ignorance, that,"
said my mother, "it's a sign of character. Pierre
will never learn the value of money."

My dear mother had read my character and my
future: she was prophesying. No, it was never to

be my fate to know the value of money. What I was·as a little boy of three or three and a half, in the little sitting-room papered with rosebuds, that I have remained till my old age, which rests lightly upon me, as it does on all who are free from avarice and pride. No, mother dear, I have never known the value of money. Even now I know it not, or perhaps I had better say that I know it too well. I know that money is the cause of all those ills that afflict our social order, which is so cruel and whereof we are so proud. That little boy whose memory I have just evoked, that little boy who, when playing his games, did not know whether it was the buyer or the seller who had to pay, sets me thinking all at once of that maker of pipes whom William Morris presents to us in that fine Utopian story of his, that simple-hearted craftsman who, in the city of the future, made pipes which surpassed all others in beauty because he brought love to the carving of them and bestowed them as gifts, taking no money in exchange.

CHAPTER IX

THE DRUM

O live is to desire. And, according as a man deems that desire is sweet or bitter, so will he regard life as good or bad. Each one of us has to decide the question for himself. Argument is useless: it is a matter of metaphysics. When I was five, I desired a drum. Was that desire sweet or bitter? I know not. Let us say that it was bitter in so far as it resulted from the lack of something, and that it was sweet inasmuch as it conjured up to my imagination the object desired.

In order that there may be no misunderstanding in the matter, let me add that I wanted to have a drum without being conscious of any desire to become a drummer. Of that calling I contemplated neither the glory nor the risks. Although fairly familiar, for my age, with the military annals of France, I had not as yet heard the story of Bara, the Drummer, who died clasping his drumsticks to his heart, or of that heroic boy of fifteen who, at the Battle of Zurich, with his arm pierced by a bullet, continued to sound the charge, was rewarded by the

First Consul with a pair of presentation drumsticks and, to prove himself worthy of them, got killed at the first opportunity. Brought up during a period of peace, I knew nothing of drummers save the two drummers of the Garde Nationale who, on New Year's Day, used to present my father, a Major in the 2nd Battalion, and his lady, with an address ornamented with a coloured picture. The picture represented the two drum majors, very much idealized, in a magnificently gilded *salon,* bowing to a gentleman in a green frock-coat and a lady wearing a crinoline and lace flounces. In reality they had roving eyes, heavy moustaches and rubicund noses. My father would give them a crown piece and send them off to drink a glass of wine which old Mélanie poured out for them in the kitchen. They would drink it down at one long draught, smack their lips and wipe their mouths on the sleeve of their tunics. Although there was a joviality about them that rather took my fancy, they never inspired me with any desire to become as one of them. No, I had no desire to be a drummer. I would rather have been a general, and, if I burned to possess a drum and a pair of black drumsticks, the reason was that I used to associate these objects with countless scenes of war.

No one could have reproached me at that time with preferring Cassandra's couch to Achilles' spear. Arms and combats were the breath of life to me. I revelled in slaughter. I had become a hero, if the fates that hamper our projects had permitted. But they did not.

The very next year they turned me aside from so glorious a path and inspired me with a love for dolls. Despite the way people tried to shame me, I bought several out of my savings. I loved them all; but I adored one above all the rest and my mother said it was not the prettiest. But why should I be in such a hurry to dim the glory of my fourth year, when all my desires were centred on a drum?

Not being endowed with a stoic's restraint, I often avowed my longing to persons able to satisfy it. They pretended not to hear, or else answered in a way that drove me to desperation.

"You know perfectly well," my mother used to say, "that your father dislikes toys that make a noise."

As she refused me out of a sense of wifely duty, I transferred my request to my Aunt Chausson, who felt no compunction in making herself disagreeable to my father. I had perceived that very clearly, and it was a circumstance on which I relied to obtain possession of the object I so ardently coveted. Unfortunately, Aunt Chausson was parsimonious. She rarely gave anything away, and not much, at that.

"What do you want with a drum?" she said. "Haven't you got toys enough? You've cupboards full of them. In my day children were not spoiled as they are now. My little playmates and I used to make dolls out of bits of paper. Haven't you got a lovely Noah's Ark?"

She was referring to a Noah's Ark which she had given me on New Year's Day, twelve months before and which, I confess, had appeared to me at first as something supernatural. It contained the patriarch and his family, and couples of all the living things in creation. But the butterflies were bigger than the elephants, and that, after a time, outraged my sense of proportion. And now that the quadrupeds, owing to my rough usage, had only got three legs to stand on, and that Noah had lost his staff, the Ark had no longer any charm for me.

One day, when I had a cold and was obliged to stay in my room with my nightcap tied under my chin, I made myself a drum out of a butter tub and a wooden spoon. It must have been a thing rather in the Dutch manner, after the style of Brauwer or Jan Steen. My tastes were more exalted, and, when my old Mélanie entered in a fume to recover possession of her butter tub and cooking spoon, I was already sick of them.

It was about that time that my father, one evening, brought me home a fancy biscuit representing a Pierrot beating a big drum. I don't know whether he thought that the image would prove a satisfactory substitute for the reality, or whether he wanted to make fun of me. He smiled, as was his wont, a little sadly. Whatever the reason, I received his present with an ill grace and the biscuit, harsh and rasping to the touch, filled me with a sudden aversion.

I had quite given up hope of ever attaining the object of my desires when, one bright summer's day, after lunch, my mother embraced me tenderly, told me to be a good boy and sent me out with Mélanie for a walk, having put into my hands an article shaped like a cylinder and wrapped in a piece of brown paper.

I opened the parcel, and, behold, it was a drum! By this time my mother had gone out of the room. I hung the beloved instrument on my shoulder by the cord which did duty for a bandoleer and raised no question as to what the fates would demand of me in return. In those days I thought that the gifts of fortune were gratis. I had not learned from Herodotus to identify the heavenly Nemesis, and I knew not the poet's adage, whereon in after years I have pondered long:

"C'est un ordre des Dieux qui jamais ne se rompt
De nous vendre bien cher les grands biens qu'ils nous font."

Happy and proud, the drum at my side, the drumsticks in my hands, I darted forth and marched in front of Mélanie, beating my drum with a gallant flourish. I marched as though to the attack, as one leading his armies to certain victory. I had a sort of feeling, though I did not avow it even to myself,

that my drum was not very sonorous and was not
to be heard three miles away. And it was the fact
that the ass's skin (if skin it were, which I greatly
doubt to-day), being loosely stretched, did not re-
sound beneath the blow of the drumsticks, which
were so slender and so light that I could not feel
them between my fingers. I recognized the peace-
loving and watchful spirit of my mother and her
zeal in banishing noisy playthings from the house.
She had already removed all the guns, pistols and
rifles, to my great regret, because I delighted in up-
roar and my soul was uplifted at the sound of de-
tonations. Doubtless no one would want to have
a silent drum. But enthusiasm makes up for every
defect. The tumult of my heart filled my ears with
the sound of glory. I seemed to hear a cadence that
made ten thousand men march onward keeping step
as one; I seemed to hear the rolling sounds that fill
men's heart with heroism and awe; I seemed to behold, in the flowering gardens of the Luxembourg
columns advancing as far as the eye could see across
illimitable plains; I conjured up the vision of horses,
cannons, gun-carriages making deep ruts in the
roads, gleaming helmets with sable streamers, fur
caps, aigrettes, plumes, lances and bayonets.

I saw, I felt, I created it all, and, in the world of
my imagination, I myself was all, the men, the
horses, the guns, the powder magazines, the fiery
heavens and the blood-stained earth. That was

what I conjured forth from my drum And my
Aunt Chausson had asked me what I wanted with a
drum!

When I returned to the house it was silent. I
called out for my mother, but she did not answer.
I ran to her bedroom and to the rosebud sitting-
room, but there was no one there. I went into my
father's study; it was empty. Standing erect on
the drawing-room clock Foyatier's *Spartacus* alone
responded to my anxious look, with his gesture of
eternal indignation.

"Mamma!" I cried, "Mamma, where are you?"
And I began to weep.

Then old Mélanie told me that my father and
mother had departed on the diligence that leaves
the Rue du Bouloi for Le Havre, with Monsieur
and Madame Danguin, and that they would be away
a week.

This announcement plunged me into the depths
of despair, and I knew at what a price Fate had
granted me a drum; I knew that my mother had
given me a toy to cover her departure and to distract my thoughts from her absence. And remem-
bering the grave and somewhat melancholy voice
in which, as she kissed me, she bade me 'Be a good
boy!" I wondered how it was I had never suspected it.

"If I had only known," I thought, "I wouldn't
have let her go."

I was sad and also ashamed at having allowed myself to be taken in. And there had been so many signs that ought to have told me what was afoot. For days past I had heard my parents whispering together, I had heard cupboard doors creaking, I had seen piles of linen on the beds, trunks and portmanteaux encumbering the rooms—the domed lid of one of the trunks was covered with a skin worn bare in patches, over which were fixed bands of very dirty black wood; it was a hideous thing. All these presages appeared to me in vain, though a wretched dog would have been disturbed by them. I had heard my father say that Finette used to know when anyone was about to go away.

The house seemed vast and cheerless. The horrible silence which reigned within it sent a chill to my heart. To fill the void Mélanie was really too little. Her fluted cap scarcely reached above my head. I loved Mélanie, I loved her with all the force of my childish egoism, but she was not sufficient to occupy my mind. Her remarks struck me as insipid. For all that her hair was grey and her back growing round, she appeared to me to be more of a child than I was. The thought of living a whole week alone with her reduced me to despair.

She tried to console me. She said that a week was soon over; that my mother would bring back a nice little boat, that I could sail it on the Luxembourg lake, that my father and mother would tell

me about all the things that happened to them on
their journey and would give me such a good description of the fine port at Le Havre that I should
fancy I was there myself. It must be adm tted that
this last touch was not without merit since the pigeon
of the fabulist employed it to console his tender con-
sort for his absence. But I refused to be comforted.
I did not think consolation was possible and I deemed
that it would detract from the nobility of my attitude.

Aunt Chausson came to dine with me. It gave
me no pleasure to behold her owlish countenance.
She also proffered consolation, but her comfort had
a flavour of old bones about it, like everything else
she gave away. Hers was too niggardly a nature
to bestow consolation in fresh and pure abundance.
At the dinner table she sat in my mother's place,
from which, therefore, no imperceptible effluence of
her could arise, no impalpable shade, no invisible
image, nothing of that mysterious essence of absent
beloved ones which lingers about the things with
which they were familiar. The incongruity of the
thing exasperated me. In my despair I refused to
eat my soup and took pride in the refusal. I don't
remember whether it occurred to me then that, in
similar circumstances, Finette would have done as
much; but, if it had, I should not have felt ashamed,
for I realized that, in matters of instinct and feeling, animals were far beyond me. My mother had

left orders that there should be a *vol-au-vent* and
some cream for dinner, thinking that these things
were calculated to take my mind off my troubles. I
had refused the soup; I accepted the *vol-au-vent* and
the cream and, in them, found some relief for my
woes.

After dinner Aunt Chausson advised me to go
and play with my Noah's Ark; this suggestion made
me blaze with fury. I answered her in a most impertinent manner and, not only that, but hurled some
very unseemly insults at Mélanie, who, in the whole
course of her saintly life, never merited aught but
praise.

Poor soul, she put me to bed with delicate care,
wiped away my tears and fixed up her own truckle-
bed in my room. Nevertheless, I was swiftly to perceive the terrible effects of the lonely state to which
my mother had abandoned me. But, properly to understand what befell me, it must be borne in mind
that, every night, in that very room, before I fell
asleep, I used to see from my bed a troop of little
men with big heads, hump-backed, bandy-legged,
curiously deformed, wearing felt hats with feathers
stuck in them, great round spectacles on their noses,
and carrying divers objects such as spigots, mando-
lins, saucepans, tambourines, saws, trumpets,
crutches, wherewith they made strange noises, tread-
ing fantastic measures. Their appearance there at
this hour had ceased to astonish me. I was not suf-

ficiently well acquainted with the laws of Nature to know that such a phenomenon was inconsistent with them; and since the same procession took place regularly, night after night, I did not regard it as extraordinary. It scared me, without, however, causing me sufficient fear to make me scream. A circumstance that greatly allayed my terror was that I noticed that these little minstrels kept very close to the wall and never came near my bed. Such was their custom. They looked as if they did not see me and I held my breath so as not to attract their attention. It was assuredly my mother's good influence that kept them away from me, but doubtless the aged Mélanie did not exert the same sway over these mischievous spirits, for on that dreadful night when the diligence of the Rue du Bouloi carried off my beloved parents to distant shores, these little musicians noticed my presence for the first time. One of them, a little personage with a wooden leg and a plaster over his eye, nudged his neighbour and pointed his finger at me and then all of them, one after another, turned to look at me, put on enormous round spectacles and examined me curiously, with no friendly expression. I began to tremble in every limb. But when they came over to my bed, dancing and brandishing spigots, saws and stewpans, and one of them, with a nose like a clarinet, pointed at me with a syringe as big round

as the telescope at the Observatory, I was frozen
with terror and called out:

"Mamma! Mamma!"

Hearing my cry, old Mélanie came running to
see what was the matter. At the sight of her I
burst into tears. Then I dropped off to sleep again.

When I awoke to the twittering of the sparrows, I
had forgotten all, the melancholy absence of my
parents and my own loneliness. Alas, my mother's
radiant face did not lean down over my bed, her
dark wavy tresses did not caress my cheeks, I did
not breathe-in the iris which perfumed her dressing-
gown. Instead, I beheld the cheeks of my old Mélanie, that resembled winter apples. She appeared to
me in an enormous night cap and I saw temples and
Cupids on the dear creature's night-gown. They
were printed in pink on a hodden-grey ground and
she wore them in perfect innocence. The sight re-
newed my grief. All the morning I wandered, dis-
consolate, about the silent dwelling. Finding my
drum on a chair in the dining-room, I threw it on
the floor in a passion, and, with a blow of my heel,
stove it in.

Later on, when I had arrived at Man's estate, it
may have chanced that I again felt a desire for something similar to that sonorous and hollow instrument for which I had longed so greatly when a little
child—for the tympana of glory or the cymbals of
popular favour. But, as soon as I felt this desire

coming to life and stirring within me, I bethought me of the drum of my childhood when I was a little boy of four, and of the price I had paid for it, and forthwith I ceased to desire the favours that destiny does not bestow on us without asking something in return.

Jean Racine, reading in his Latin Bible, underlined the following passage: *Et tribuit eis petitionem eorum,* and he recalled it when he put into the mouth of Aricie those words which bring a pallor to the cheek of the imprudent Theseus:

"Craignez, seigneur, craignez que le ciel rigoureux
Ne vous haïsse assez pour exaucer vos vœux.
Souvent dans sa colère il reçoit nos victimes:
Ses présents sont souvent la peine de nos crimes."

CHAPTER X

COMEDY WELL HANDLED

N those days, when I lay sleepless in bed because I was out of sorts, or simply because I had awakened earlier than usual, I used to be conscious that an ashen and dismal countenance was gazing at me, a countenance vast and indeterminate of outline, a phantom, in short, more dreadful than pain or fear. It was the thing we call Ennui. Not tthe sort of heart-ache whereof the poets sing, a heart-ache tinged with the hues of hatred or of love, a heart-ache high-sorrowful and splendid; no, not that, but the dull, monotonous, fathomless ennui, the fog within, emptiness grown visible. To banish this spectral intruder I would call for my mother and for Mélanie. Alas, they came not, or if they came, they stayed but a moment at my side, and said to me, as the bee remarked to Madame Des-bordes-Valmore's little boy:

> "Je suis très pressée,
> On ne rit pas toujours."

And my mother would add the recommendation that I should just run through my multiplication table to pass away the time.

That was an extreme measure that I was loath to adopt. My tastes lay rather in the direction of pretending I was making a voyage round the world and taking part in extraordinary adventures. I used to get shipwrecked and to swim ashore to an island inhabited by lions and tigers. With a powerful imagination to back me, that ought to have been enough to keep ennui at bay. But unfortunately the pictures I conjured up were so colourless and insubstantial that they hid neither the wall paper of my room nor the misty countenance that I abhorred. As time went on, I did better and succeeded in providing myself, as I lay in my cot, with a pastime as agreeable as it was witty and, moreover, one very much in vogue among civilized communities: I played me a comedy. My theatre, I need hardly say, did not attain perfection all at once. Greek tragedy, it will be remembered, had its origin in the bucolic wain of Thespis. I used to hum tunes, beating time with my hand. Such was the origin of my Odeon. It was of lowly birth. A kindly attack of measles kept me in bed that I might bring it to perfection. I had five actors to look after, or rather five characters, like those of the Italian comedy. They were the five fingers of my right hand. Each had his own name as well as his distinctive physiognomy. And after the manner of the masks of the Italian theatre on the resemblance to which I cannot too greatly insist, my *dramatis personæ* kept

their names in the rôles they played, unless of course
the piece made a change obligatory, as sometimes
happened, in historic dramas for example. But they
invariably retained their characters. In this respect,
and I am not flattering them, they were never found
wanting.

The thumb was called Rappart. Why? you ask.
I cannot tell. We must not expect to clear up every
mystery. It is impossible to explain everything.
Rappart was a short, broad, thick-set fellow of
prodigious strength; an uneducated, violent, quarrelsome, besotted creature, a regular Caliban, black-
smith, porter, pantechnicon man, brigand, soldier,
according to the part he was playing. Everything
he did was violent and cruel. When need arose
he took the part of savage beasts, such as the wolf
in *Little Red Riding Hood,* or of the bear in a rather
nice comedy in which a young shepherdess comes
upon a white bear fast asleep, slips a ring through
his nose and leads him captive and capering to the
palace of the King, who weds her forthwith.

The index finger, whose name was Mitoufle, presented a striking contrast to Rappart both in appearance and mentality. Mitoufle was neither the
tallest nor the handsomest of the troop. Indeed, he
seemed a little defective and deformed by some
manual labour undertaken at too tender an age. But
for vivacity of movement and talent for repartee he
was the best of my actors. Nature had endowed

him with a big heart and his first impulse was to
hasten to succour the oppressed.   His courage was
carried to the point of rashness and the dramatist
gave him plenty of opportunities to display it.   He
hadn't a rival, when a house was on fire, in snatching
a baby from the flames and restoring it to its mother.
His sole defect was an excess of sprightliness.   But
for that we forgave him, or rather we loved him
the better for it.

"Achille déplairait moins bouillant et moins prompt."

The middle finger, elegant, upright, tall and proud
of mien, harboured, beneath his charming exterior,
a chivalrous soul.   Descended from the most illustrious ancestry, he was called Dunois.   And in this
instance I've a strong notion that I know how he
came by his name.   I don't think there is much room
for doubt that my mother was the cause.   My dear
mother was not a very good singer and she only
sang when there was no one save me to listen.   She
used to sing:

"Partant pour la Syrie
Le jeune et beau Dunois
Alla prier Marie
De bénir ses exploits."

She also sang *Reposez-vous, bons chevaliers*.   Nay,
and she sang too, *En soupirant, j'ai vu naître l'au-
rore*.   My dear mother thought a tremendous lot of
the ballads of Queen Hortense, which were considered charming in those days.

Excuse me for going so slowly; but it is a whole

art that I am setting forth. The ring-finger, which bore no ring, was identified with a lady of great beauty named Blanche of Castille. It was very likely a pseudonym. Being the only woman in the troop, she took the part of mothers, wives and sweethearts. Virtuous and persecuted, she was rescued times without number from the greatest perils by the young and handsome Dunois, with the eager and unselfish assistance of Mitoufle. She often married Dunois, rarely Mitoufle. One more character and I shall have finished with my troop. Jeannot, the little finger, was a very innocent small boy, who, when necessary, became a girl, as, for example, when the piece was *Little Red Riding Hood.* And I think that, when he turned into a girl, his wits grew sharper.

The plays designed for the interpreters whom I have just enumerated resembled the *commedia del arte* in this respect, namely, that I composed the canvas and my actors improvised the dialogue, adapting their language to their characters and situations. In all other respects, however, they differed widely from the Italian farce and the pieces enacted in booths at country fairs where Harlequin, Columbine and the Doctor engage in rivalry for sordid interests and ignoble passions. My works were cast in a nobler mould and appertained to the heroic order, as befits the innocent and the simple-hearted. I was lyrical and I was pathetic, tragic and very tragic. When passion soared to heights beyond the scope of mortal speech, I had recourse to song. My dramas also had their comic scenes. Thus all unwittingly I composed in the Shakespearean manner. I should have found it much harder to have imitated Racine. Unlike M. de Lamartine, I had no rooted detestation of buffoonery. Far from it; but my comic scenes were very simple, without any admixture of irony. The same situations were often repeated in my theatre. I hadn't the heart to take myself to task on that account; they were so touching! Captive princesses set free by valiant knights, children kidnapped and restored to their mothers, these were the subjects I loved best.

Nevertheless, I traced out other stories besides these. I composed love dramas, lavishly supplied with ladies of conspicuous beauty. These plays, however, were deficient in action and, more especially, lacking in *dénouement*. These defects really resulted from my purity of mind, for, looking on love as in itself its own sufficient reward, I did not consider that it demanded any further satisfaction. It was fine, but rather tedious.

I also dealt with warlike subjects and was not afraid to tackle the story of Napoleon, which I gathered from the lips of survivors of those glorious times, for they were numerous about me in my childhood days. Dunois used to be Napoleon; Blanche of Castille was Joséphine (I knew nothing about Marie-Louise); Mitoufle, a grenadier; Jean-

not, a fifer. Rappart represented the English, the
Prussians, the Austrians and the Russians, that is
to say, the enemy. And these resources sufficed me
to win the battles of Austerlitz, Jena, Friedland and
Wagram and to make a triumphal entry into Vienna
and Berlin. As a rule, I did not give the same piece
twice over. I always had a play ready. For fer-
tility I was a veritable Calderon.

It will readily be appreciated that, thanks to the
diversions of this theatre in which I was at once
manager, author, actors and audience, I did not have
such a bad time of it in bed. Indeed, I used to remain there as long as I could and pretended to be
suffering from all sorts of ailments in order not to
have to get up. My dear mamma, who did not know
me for the same boy, asked me how it was I had
grown so lazy all of a sudden. Not understanding
my art or taking the measure of my genius, she
applied the term laziness to what was in fact action
and movement.

This theatre, having attained its zenith about my
sixth year, fell suddenly into a rapid decline whereof
it behoves me to explain the cause. When I was
about six years old, some indisposition incidental
to childhood kept me several days in bed and, having at my side a little table, a box of paints and
some pieces of ribbon, I decided to employ the
means thus ready to my hand in embellishing my
theatre and in bringing it to a state of perfection

hitherto undreamt of. I set to work at once and
carried out with ardour the feverish conceptions of
my imagination. It had never struck me that none
of my actors had anything more in the way of physiognomy than an egg. Suddenly becoming aware of
this defect, I made them eyes, noses, mouths and,
perceiving that they were nude, I attired them in
raiment of silk and gold. It next occurred to me
that they ought to have something on their heads
and I made them hats or bonnets of divers shapes
but for the most part pointed. I never wearied in
my quest after picturesque effect. I built a stage,
painted scenery, and manufactured accessories. In
an access of great emotion I produced a play en-
titled, "The Knights of the Holy Sepulchre," in
which East and West were to encounter one another
in a formidable combat. Alas, I couldn't even get
through the first scene. The well-spring of inspiration had been frozen; soul and movement, all had
disappeared. No more passion, no more life. My
theatre, so long as it had remained independent of
artifice, had put on all the hues and all the shapes
of illusion. When luxury appeared on the scene,
illusion faded away. The Muses took wing. They
never came back. What a lesson was there! Art
must be allowed to retain its noble nudity. Rich
dresses and brilliant scenery stifle drama, whose sole
adornment should consist in the grandeur of the
action and the truth of the characters.

CHAPTER XI

THE LINT MAKERS

 HAD not yet completed my fourth year, when, one morning, my mother took me out of my bed and my dear papa, who had put on his National Guard's uniform, embraced me tenderly. On his shako he had a golden cock and a crimson tuft. Down on the quay the drums were beating to arms. The noise of galloping horses resounded along the cobbled street. From time to time there came the sound of singing and uproarious shouting and in the distance the rattle of musketry. My father went out. My mother went to the window, drew aside the muslin curtain and fell a-sobbing. It was the Revolution.

I have but a scanty recollection of those February days. I was never once taken out while the street fighting went on. Our windows looked on to the courtyard and the events which were taking place in the outer world were, for me, infinitely mysterious. All the tenants began to fraternize with each other. Madame Caumont, the wife of the bookseller and publisher; Mademoiselle

Mathilde, the daughter, already well on in years, of
Madame Laroque; Mademoiselle Cécile, the dressmaker; the very elegant Madame Petitpas; the beautiful Madame Moser who, in ordinary times, used
to get the cold shoulder from every one, all fore-
gathered at my mother's to make bandages for the
wounded, whose numbers increased every minute.
The custom then followed in all the hospitals was
to apply linen threads to the wounds, and no one
entertained any doubts as to the wisdom of this treatment until a revolution in surgery prescribed the ap-
plication of moist dressings. Each of these ladies
brought her parcel of linen. They sat in the dining-
room round the circular table and tore the linen
into narrow strips which they then proceeded to un-
ravel. It was wonderful, when one comes to think
of it, what a quantity of old linen these housewives
possessed. On a piece of an old shirt which she had
brought with her, Madame Petitpas deciphered the
monogram of her maternal grandmother and the
date 1745. Mamma took part in the work with her
guests. We, young Octave Caumont and myself,
likewise bore a hand in this labour of mercy, under
the controlling eye of old Mélanie who, with her
toil-hardened hands was unravelling muslin, sitting,
out of deference to the company, a foot or two away
from the table. For myself, I was acquitting myself
of my task with zeal, and my pride went on increasing with every thread I drew out. But, when I per-

ceived that Octave Caumont's pile was bigger than mine, my *amour-propre* was wounded and my satisfaction at preparing these comforts for the wounded suffered a sensible abatement.

From time to time some good friend of ours, M. Debas, surnamed Simon de Nantua, or M. Caumont, the publisher, would come in and tell us how matters were progressing.

M. Caumont had on the uniform of the National Guard, but he was far from wearing it with the elegance of my dear papa. My papa's complexion was pale and his figure slender and graceful. M. Caumont had a puffy, rubicund countenance, and the folds of a triple chin reposed upon his tunic front. Moreover, he was too fat to get it to, and it gaped ingloriously over the stomach part.

"Things are in a terrible state," he said. "Paris in flames, the streets bristling with seven hundred barricades, the mob besieging the Château, Marshal Bugeaud defending it with four thousand men and six pieces of artillery."

These tidings were received with the liveliest manifestations of terror and pity. The aged Mélanie, seated apart from the rest, kept making the sign of the cross and moving her lips in silent prayer.

My mother ordered sherry and biscuits to be put on the table. (Tea was very seldom drunk in those days, and ladies were more accustomed to drink wine

than they are now.)   A sip of sherry brought a
sparkle to their eyes and a smile to their lips.   You
wouldn't have thought they were the same faces, or
the same people.

While refreshments were being taken, M. Clérot,
carver and gilder of the Quai Malaquais, presented
himself before us.   He was a very stout man, far
stouter than M. Caumont, and his white blouse made
him look rounder than ever.   He bowed to the company, and begged that Dr. Nozière would come to
the Palais Royal and see to the wounded who were
lying there helpless and neglected.   My mother replied that Dr. Nozière was at the Charity Hospital.
M. Clérot gave us a terrible account of what he had
seen near the Tuileries.   Dead and wounded all
about the place, horses with one leg broken, or with
gaping wounds in their bellies, trying to get on their
feet and falling down again, and notwithstanding all
that, the cafés filled with people out to see what they
could see, and a group of street arabs making game
of a dog that was howling beside a corpse.   He told
how the guard-house of the Château-d'Eau, be-
sieged by a heavy column of rebels equipped with
arms and munitions, was enveloped in flames, and
how its defenders at length laid down their arms.

M. Clérot continued his narrative somewhat as
follows:

"After the surrender of the guard, volunteers
were called for to help put the fire out.   I happened

to be among the number; we procured some buckets
and formed up in a line. I was stationed about fifty
paces from the burning mass between a respectable
middle-aged citizen and a slip of a boy who was
wearing a military cartridge box slung over his
shoulder. The buckets were passed to and fro.
'Steady, there, citizens!' said I. 'Steady!' I was
not feeling very well. The wind was blowing the
flames and the smoke right in our faces. My feet
were as cold as ice, and every now and then I felt
a deathly chill pass right down my leg. I tried to
discover the cause, but could not. At last I began
to wonder whether I had been wounded in the combat without noticing it, and was losing all my blood,
and as I stood there in the line I said to myself,
'This feeling isn't natural,' and I looked in front,
behind, right and left, to find out what was happen-
ing to me. But would you believe it, all of a sudden
I caught my left-hand neighbour, the boy, busily
emptying the contents of the bucket I had just passed
to him, into the pocket of my blouse. Ladies, the
young rascal got a beautiful box on the ears, and I
hope he will go and show it to his lady-love. And
now, if you *would* be so kind, Madame Nozière, I
should be very glad to warm myself for a minute or
two by your fire. The young beggar has chilled me
to the bone. It's enough to make you shudder to
think that youngsters nowadays don't know better
than to behave like that."

And the obese gentleman, having extracted from
his pocket a three-foot rule, a glazier's diamond, and
a newspaper reduced to a paste, turned it inside out
all dripping with water.   He pulled up his blouse,
and soon his clothes began to steam in the heat of
the fire.   My mother poured him out a glass of
brandy, which he drank to the health of the company, for he knew his manners.   I thought t all tre-
mendously exciting, and I plainly saw Madame Caumont making frantic endeavours to prevent herself
exploding with laughter. .

At this juncture, M. Debas, surnamed Simon de
Nantua, appeared on the scene, rifle in hand.   He
was wearing his belt and shoulder-straps buckled on
over his frock coat.   He bore himself with an air of
extreme importance, and in tones of great solemnity
informed Madame Nozière that the doctor was de-
tained at the hospital, and would not be home to
dinner.   He told us all about the things he had seen
or heard, devoting himself chiefly to the events in
which he had personally participated: six municipal
guards chased by the rebels and concealed by him in
a cellar in the Rue de Beaune; a royal outrider,
whose scarlet coat would have made him a certain
victim of the infuriated populace, taken by him to a
wine shop at the corner of the Rue de Verneuil and
there disguised in a cellarman's overall.   He told us
that Firmin, M. Bellaguet's valet, had just been
killed on the quay by a stray bullet; and, as we are

principally moved by the things which happen in our own neighbourhood, this last piece of news upset us all greatly.

I also remember that a little while later, when darkness had come on and I was at Madame Caumont's with my dear mamma, I peered through the entresol window, which looked on to the quay, and saw a cart piled with a very tall and bulky freight coming through the gates of the Louvre, all on fire. A lot of men dragged it along on to the Pont des Saints-Pères between the two-seated statues, and when they reached the middle of the bridge they tipped it up. It rebounded twice on its springs, and then, carrying away the cast-iron railings, toppled over into the Seine. This sight, which was suddenly followed by utter darkness, struck me as splendid and mysterious.

Those are my recollections of the 24th. February, 1848, as they impressed themselves on my childish mind, and as my mother has time and again recalled them to me. There you have them in their naked artlessness. I have been very careful not to dress them up, not to add any sort of embellishment.

The manner in which I then became acquainted with current events permanently influenced my attitude towards public life and went a long way towards building up my philosophy of history. In my earliest childhood, French people had a sense of the ludicrous which, under the influences of causes

that I am unable to define, they have since lost.
In pamphlet, in picture, and in song, their mocking
spirit was manifest. I was born in the golden age
of caricature, and it was from the lithographs of the
Charivari and the quips of my godfather, M. Pierre
Danquin, a typical Paris bourgeois, that I acquired
my ideas of national life. It struck me as comic, in
spite of the riots and revolutions amid which I was
brought up. My godfather used to call Louis Napoleon Bonaparte the moping parrot. I used to delight in picturing this bird as doing battle with the
Red Terror, the Red Terror being represented as a
scarecrow tied to the end of a broom handle. And
round about them I saw the Orleanists with pear-
shaped heads, M. Thiers as a dwarf, Girardin as a
Merry Andrew, and President Dupin with a face
like a colander and shoes as big as boats. But I was
especially interested in Victor Considérant who, I
knew, lived close by, on the Quai Voltaire, and who
appeared to me as hanging from the branches of
trees by a long tail, with a great big eye at the tip
of it.

CHAPTER XII

THE TWO SISTERS

T that time, my mamma frequently took me down the Rue du Bac. Winter was coming on, and in that busy street she purchased knitted things and all sorts of woollen garments, and ordered a warm suit for me from M. Augris, a tailor equally notable for his courtesy and his incompetence. His shop was opposite the house where M. de Chateaubriand had died the year before. This consideration affected me but little, and I glanced but casually at the doorway, adorned with medallions in a chaste and dignified style, which had opened to let him pass out never to return. What especially delighted me in the beautiful Rue du Bac were the shops full of objects marvellous in form and colour, tapestry in infinite variety, note-paper with letters engraved in gold and azure, lions and panthers figured on bed hangings, heads modelled in wax with the hair most beautifully dressed, Savoy biscuits of which the dome, like the dome of the Pantheon, was surmounted by a full blown rose; then, too, there were wondrous little pastries in the

shape of three-cornered hats and dominoes and man-
dolins. As she showed me these marvels, my mother
added a word or two that made them more marvellous still, for she had the rare gift of giving everything a soul and of infusing mere symbols with life.

At the corner of this street and the Rue de l'Uni-
versité, there used to live a picture-dealer, the entrance to whose shop was through a somewhat narrow doorway painted yellow and decorated in the
contemporary manner, with a certain richness of
ornamentation. Of the cornice which surmounted
it, I can say nothing, for I have no recollection of it,
but it is certain that, leaning their backs against the
two consoles which supported that cornice, there
were two little figures about as long as one's arm,
weirdly partaking of the characteristics of man,
bird, and beast. They were not, strictly speaking,
chimeras, for they in no way proceeded from the
lion or the goat, nor were they griffins, since they
had a woman's breasts. Long ears stuck up from
their heads, which were something like a bat's. Their
thin, lithe bodies were of the greyhound order. On
the lamp brackets of the Pont de Suresnes, there are
some fantastic little creatures somewhat resembling
them, and they were also a little like a monster that
supported a lantern on the façade of the Palazzo
Riccardi at Florence. As a matter of fact, they were
little decorative figures executed somewhere about
the year 1840 by Feuchère, or one of his school, but

they were endowed with a very singular physiognomy, and they fill much too important a place in my life for me to mix them up with any other carving of a similar description.

My mother it was who pointed them out to me one day as we were passing by.

"Pierre, look at those little creatures," she said. "They have a lot of expression. Their faces are full of gaiety and mischief. One could look at them for hours together, so sprightly and so full of life they seem."

I asked what their names were. My mother replied that they had no names in Natural History because they did not exist in Nature.

"They are the two sisters," I said.

We had to go back next day for M. Augris to try on my winter suit again. As we passed by the two sisters, my dear mamma gravely pointed them out to me with her finger.

"Look," said she, "they are not laughing now."

And mamma spoke truly.

The expression of the two sisters had changed. They laughed no more. They had a grim and threatening aspect.

I asked why they had ceased to laugh.

"Because you have not been a good boy to-day."

There was no gainsaying that. I had not been good that day. I had gone into the kitchen, whither my heart ever impelled me to go, and where I had found old Mélanie peeling turnips. I wanted to peel them, too, or rather to carve them, for I meditated moulding them into the shapes of men and animals. Mélaine objected. Annoyed at her opposition, I clutched hold of her goffered cap with its lace wings, and tore it off her head. A wild impulsive genius might have done a thing like that; it was certainly not the deed of a good boy. I turned my gaze on the two sisters, and, whether it was that they really did appear to me to be endowed with supernatural power, or whether it was that my mind, hungering after the marvellous, assisted the illusion, a little shiver of fear, half joy, half terror, made my heart quake.

"They do not know the naughty things you have done," said my mother, "but you may read them in their eyes. Be good and they will smile upon you, they and all Nature with them."

Since then, every time we passed by the two sisters, my mother and I, we scanned them anxiously, to see whether their faces were wrathful or serene, and always their expression corresponded exactly with the state of my conscience. I consulted them in the fullness of faith, and found in their countenance, whether smiling or sombre, the recompense of my good behaviour, or the penalty of my misdeeds.

Long years slipped by. Having attained to nan's estate and complete intellectual emancipation, I still used to consult the two sisters in hours of perplexity and irresolution. One day, when I had a special need to read clearly within my heart, I went to ask them for guidance. They were no longer to be seen. They had disappeared, together with the door that they adorned. I departed filled with doubt and hesitation, and forthwith committed **an error of judgment.**

CHAPTER XIII

CATHERINE AND MARIANNE

HE sea, when I saw it for the first time, only impressed me with its vastness by reason of the infinite sadness which it brought into my heart as I gazed upon it and breathed its salt savour. It was the sea, wild and untamed. We had come to spend one of the summer months at a little village in Brittany, and one aspect of the coast is graven, as though with an etcher's needle, on my memory, and that was the sight of a row of trees beaten by the sea wind and stretching, beneath a lowering sky, their bowed trunks and withered branches towards the flat, barren soil.

It was a sight that ate itself into my heart. It lingers with me as the symbol of some unparalleled misfortune.

The sounds and scents of the sea haunted and troubled me. Every day and every hour, the sea seemed to me to undergo a change, now sleek and blue, now overspread with tiny, gentle wavelets, blue on one side, silvery on the other, now seemingly hidden beneath a sheet of polished green canvas, now

heavy and sombre and bearing on its tossing crests
the tameless herds of Nereus; yesterday coy and
smiling; to-day tumultuous and threatening. Little
child as I was, and indeed because I was but a poor
little child, this treacherous instability greatly les-
sened the confidence and affection wherewith Nature
inspired me. The living things of the sea, fish that
swam, fish that dwelt in shells, and especially the
crustaceous creatures, were more terrifying than the
monsters that gathered round St. Anthony in the
hour of his temptation, monsters which I had been
wont to examine with such curiosity on Madame
Letord's stall, on my own Quai Malaquais. Those
crayfish, octopuses, star-fish, and crabs told me of
forms of life that were too dreadfully uncanny,
creatures that assuredly had less of brotherly love
about them than my little dog Caire, than Madame
Caumont's pony, than Robinson Crusoe's asses, than
the Paris sparrows, less of friendliness than the lions
in my picture Bible, and the animals in my Noah's
Ark. These denizens of the deep pursued me even
in my dreams, and came to me, by night, vague and
vast in their horny coverings of bluish black, prickly
and hairy, armed with pincers and saws, without
faces, and more terrifying on that account than on
any other.

The very next day after my arrival, I was enrolled
by a big boy in a troop of children who, furnished
with picks and shovels, built a sand castle on the

beach, planted the French flag thereon, and defended
it against the advancing tide. We were defeated
with honour. I was one of the last to quit the dis-
mantled fort, having done my duty, but accepting
defeat with a ready acquiescence that scarcely betokened a warlike spirit.

One day I went out in a boat with Jean Élô to
catch shell-fish. Jean Élô had light blue eyes. His
face was tanned and sun cured, and his hands so
rough that they scraped my own when he took hold
of them to show his love for me. He went out to sea
to catch fish, he mended his nets, he caulked his boat,
and occupied his spare time in building a fully rigged
schooner in a water bottle. Though he was but little
given to talking, he told me his history, which consisted solely of descriptions of the death of his rela-
tives and connections who had perished at sea. His
father and three of his brothers had all been
drowned together the winter before, wherein, as in
everything else that happened, he saw naught but
good. What religion I possessed led me to regard
Jean Élô as one gifted with celestial wisdom. One
Sunday evening we discovered him lying on the path
dead drunk, and we were obliged to step over him.
He was none the less perfect in my eyes. Perhaps
the sentiment arose from a leaning towards Quiet-
ism on my part. But I leave that for others to de-
cide; theology was not my strong point in those days;
it is a good deal less so to-day.

My dearest delight was to go shrimping with two
little girls who inspired me with a fairylike and fleeting affection. One of them, Marianne Le Guerrec,
was the daughter of a Quimper lady, with whom
my mother had struck up an acquaintance on the
beach; the other, Catherine O'Brien, was Irish.
Both of them had fair hair and blue eyes. They
were very much alike, which need not excite surprise:

"Car les vierges d'Erin et les vierges d'Armor
Sont des fruits détachés du même rameau d'or."

Prompted by a secret, instinctive grace to inter-
weave their movements, they were always to be seen
arm linked in arm or hand clasped in hand. Keeping time with their slender bare legs bronzed by the
sun and sea water, they raced along the sand, turning and twisting as though weaving some mazy
dance. Catherine O'Brien was the prettier of the
two, but she spoke French badly, and that puzzled
me somewhat. I looked for pretty shells to give
them, and these they disdained. I went out of my
way to do them little services which they either pretended not to notice or to be overcome by them.
When I looked at them they turned away their heads,
but if, in turn, I feigned not to see them, they attracted my attention by some prank or other. They
used to make me nervous, and at their approach I
forgot all the things I had intended to say to them.
If I spoke to them roughly sometimes, it was due to
fear or spite or some inexplicable perversity. Mari-

anne and Catherine were at one in making fun of
the little girl bathers of their own age. On all other
matters they were more often quarrelling than not.
They made it a mutual grievance that they had not
been born in the same country. Marianne bitterly
reproached Catherine for being English. Catherine,
who hated England, flared up at the insult, stamped
her foot, ground her teeth, and cried that she was
Irish. But Marianne didn't see the difference. One
day, in Madame O'Brien's bungalow, they came to
blows about their respective countries. Marianne
came to us on the beach with her face all scratches.

"Goodness gracious, what has happened to you?"
exclaimed her mother when she saw her.

Marianne's reply was very simple:

"Catherine teased me because I am French, and
so I called her an ugly English thing, and gave her
a punch on the nose and made it bleed. Madame
O'Brien sent us both up to Catherine's room to wash,
and we made it up because there was only one basin
between us."

CHAPTER XIV

THE UNKNOWN WORLD

VERY day, when lunch was over, old Mélanie went up to her attic and put on her flat shiny shoes, tied the strings of her white lace bonnet before her glass, wrapped her little black shawl across her chest, and fastened it with a pin. She performed all these things with studious attention to detail, for, in every department of activity, art is difficult, and Mélanie left nothing to chance in respect of those things which she deemed calculated to render the human body respectable, seemly, and worthy of its divine origin. Satisfied at length that she had befittingly attended to all the externals required of her sex, age and condition, she locked the door of her room, went downstairs with me, stopped dumbfounded in the hall, gave vent to a loud exclamation, and hurried upstairs again to her garret to fetch her bag, which she had left behind, in accordance with her long established custom. She would never have been prevailed upon to go out without the red velvet bag which contained her everlasting knitting, and from which she would pull out her scissors, needle and thread when she needed them, from which, too, on one occasion she had produced a little square piece of court plaster to put on my finger which was bleeding. She still kept in this bag of hers a sou with a hole in it, one of my first teeth, and her address written on a scrap of paper, in order, she said, that, if she dropped down dead in the street, she might not be taken to the Morgue. Whenever, having reached the quay, we turned to the left, we always used to go and say "How do you do?" to Madame Petit, the spectacle-seller. Madame Petit had her establishment in the open air, alongside the wall of the Hôtel de Chimay, and there she sat by her glass-case, on a high wooden chair, bolt upright and motionless, her face seared by the sun and frost, in an attitude of gloomy austerity. The two women would exchange remarks which varied little from one meeting to another, doubtless because they related to the basic and unchanging facts of human nature.

They spoke of children suffering from whooping cough or croup, of children wasting away with low fever; of women and their more mysterious ailments; of workmen cut off by terrible accidents. They spoke of the ill effects of the changing seasons on one's health; of the high cost of victuals; of the growing rapacity of men, who, as a class, were getting worse and worse every day, and of the fearful number of crimes that filled the world with horror.

I observed later on, when I came to read Hesicd, that the spectacle-seller of the Quai Malaquais thought and spoke even as the old gnomic poets of Greece.

So far from exciting my admiration, this wisdcm bored me beyond measure, and I tugged my nurse by the skirt in order to get away from it. If, however, on reaching the quay, we turned to the right instead of to the left, I was always ready to stop and look at the pictures which Madame Letord used to display along by a wooden fence which enclosed the piece of waste ground on which the Palais des Beaux-Arts now stands. These pictures filled me with wonder and admiration. Above all *Napoleon's Farewell at Fontainebleau; The Creation of Eve; The Mountain shaped like a man's head* and *The Death of Virginie,* awoke in me an emotion that even now, after all these years, has not completely subsided. But old Mélanie pulled me along and would not let me linger, either because she did not think me of a proper age to examine all these pictures or, which is more probable, because she herself could make nothing of them; for the fact is that she paid no more heed to them than did our little dog Caire.

We went sometimes to the Tuileries, sometimes to the Luxembourg. When the weather was mild and fine, we extended our walk as far as the Jardin des Plantes or the Trocadéro, in those days a lonely hill beside the Seine, grassy and flower bedecked. There

were some lucky days when they took me to play in
M. de La B's garden, permission to go there being
granted me during the owner's absence. This garden was cool and sequestered, and was planted with
tall trees. It was situated at the back of a fine
house in the Rue Saint-Dominique. I brought with
me a wooden spade about the size of my hand, and
when it was the time of year for the plane-trees to
shed their smooth, thin bark, and when, at the bottom of their trunks, the mould had been softened by
the rain and streaked with little winding furrows
which became ravines and precipices in my imagination, I spanned them with little wooden bridges, and,
at their edge, built villages, ramparts, and churches
fashioned from the slender bark. I brought blades
of grass and branches to represent trees, and laid out
gardens, avenues and forests. And I was well
pleased with my handiwork.

Those walks in city and suburb sometimes seemed
to me tedious and monotonous, sometimes exciting,
sometimes irksome, occasionally delightful and full
of gaiety. Ranging over wide tracts, we used to go
down that long avenue bravely bordered by shops
where they sold gingerbread, sticks of barley sugar,
penny whistles, paper kites, the Champs-Élysées, to
wit, where there were goat carriages too, and
wooden horses revolving to the sound of the steam
organ, and Guignol, in his theatre, doing battle with
the Devil; and then we would find ourselves on dirty

wharves with cranes busily unloading cargoes of
stone, while on the towing path horses tugged away
at heavy barges. Scene followed scene, landscape
succeeded landscape, populous or deserted, barren
or cultivated; but there was one region into whose
confines I longed beyond all others to penetrate, one
which, at certain moments, I thought I was on the
point of attaining, but which I reached never. I
knew nothing about this region, and yet I was sure
that when I beheld it I should recognize it. I did
not picture it as fairer or more pleasant than the
places I knew already—quite the reverse—but as
something completely different, and it was my ardent
ambition to discover it. This region, this world,
which I felt to be inaccessible yet near at hand, was
not that divine world whereof my mother taught me.
For me that world, the spiritual world, was strangely co-mingled in my mind with the world of sense.
God the Father, Jesus, the Blessed Virgin, the Angels, the Saints, the souls in Paradise, the souls in
Purgatory, the demons, and the damned, all these
had no mystery. I knew their story, everywhere I
encountered faces that were like to them. The Rue
Saint-Sulpice alone provided me with hundreds of
examples. No, the world which excited my uncontrollable curiosity, the world of my dreams, was a
world unknown, gloomy and silent, the mere idea of
which caused me to feel a thrill of terror. My legs
were, in all conscience, little enough to carry me

thither, and my old nurse Mélanie, at whose skirt I
pulled so eagerly, could only trot along pit-a-pat
with feeble little steps. Albeit I did not lose heart;
I clung to the hope that one day I should cross the
confines of that country which I sought with longing
and with awe. Sometimes, and in some places, it
seemed to me that a few more steps would bring me
to the land of my desire. To pull Mélanie along
with me, I had recourse to stratagem or violence,
and, when the sainted creature was for turning
home again, I would drag her furiously toward the
mysterious frontiers at the risk of tearing her dress.
And as she could make nothing of my divine frenzy,
wondering what was amiss with my heart or with
my mind, she would raise her eyes brimming with
tears to heaven. Nevertheless, I could not tell her
why I acted so; I could not cry aloud, "One step
more and we shall pass within the nameless realm."
Alas, how many times since then have I been compelled to devour within me the secret of my longing!

Assuredly, I drew for myself no mental chart of
the Unknown Land. I knew not its geography, but
I thought that I could tell some places where that
mysterious world impinged upon our own, and those
confines, as I deemed, were not far removed from
the places where I lived and had my being. I know
not by what sign I recognized them unless it was by
a certain strangeness, a certain disturbing charm
about them, and a feeling of curiosity not unmingled

with fear with which they inspired me. One of these border lines which I had never been able to pass beyond was marked by two houses united by an iron grille. They were not like other houses, but were built of great stone blocks, heavy looking, and melancholy, and girt about with a noble frieze of female figures standing hand in hand between silent escutcheons. And there in truth, if not the gateway of the material world, was situated, at all events, one of those barriers of Paris erected in the reign of Louis XVI by Ledoux, the architect, to wit, the Barrière d'Enfer.*

In the humid regions of the Tuileries, not far from the spot where the marble boar sits beneath the shade of the chestnut-trees, beneath the terrace by the waterside, there is a cool cavern wherein a white woman lies sleeping, a serpent coiled about her arm. I used to suspect that this cavern communicated with the Unknown World, but that to descend therein it was necessary to raise a heavy stone.

In the cellars of the very house in which I lived, there was a door, the sight of which thrilled me with fear and expectancy. It was nearly the same in appearance as the doors of the adjoining cellars; the lock was rusty, the woodlice glistened upon the threshold and in the crevices of the rotting woodwork, but, unlike the other doors, no one ever came

* Place d'Enfer, by a wretched pun, in the manner of the Marquis de Bièvre, became known in 1879 as Place Denfert-Rochereau.

to open it.   It is ever thus with the doors of mystery;
they are never unlocked.   And then, in the room
where I used to sleep, there rose up from the crevices between the boards, forms, nay, not forms,
shadows, nay not even shadows, influences rather,
emanations, which overwhelmed me with terror, and
could not but come from that world that was so
near and withal so inaccessible.   Perhaps the meaning of what I am saying now will not be clear.   At
the moment it is to myself alone that I am speaking,
and for once I listen to what I have to say with interest, ay, and with emotion.

Despairing sometimes of ever discovering the Unknown World for myself, I longed at least to hear
tell about it.   One day, when Mélanie was seated
with her knitting on one of the chairs in the Luxembourg, I asked her if she knew anything about what
existed in the cave where the white woman lay asleep
with the serpent coiled about her arm, or of what
was behind that cellar door which never, never
opened.

She seemed not to understand me.

But I returned to the charge:

"And the two houses of the stone woman, what is
there after you have passed them?"

Getting no reply, I gave another turn to my questions:

"Mélanie, tell me a tale of the Unknown Land."
Mélanie smiled.

"Mon petit monsieur," she said. "I know no tale of the Unknown Land."

As I insisted and grew importunate:

"Mon petit monsieur, I will sing you a song." And under her breath she hummed so softly you could hardly hear her:

> "Compère Guilleri,
> Te lairreras-tu mourí'?"

Alas, Life, that Queen of Metamorphoses, has suffered me to remain like to the child which asked his nurse to tell him the things that no man knoweth! I have dragged a long chain of days without giving up the hope of finding the Unknown Land.

Whithersoever I have wandered, I have sought for it. Ah, many a time and oft, beside the silver waters of the Gironde, as I roamed the billowy ocean of the vines with my comrade, my friend, the little brown dog Mitzi, many a time and oft, have I trembled, at a turning in the track, as I came upon a pathway unexplored. Thou hast seen me, Mitzi, scanning the crossways, every corner of the road, every winding of the woodland track, thinking to behold that dread apparition, formless, like to the uncreate, which would have for a moment relieved me of the burthen of the mystery, the heavy and the weary weight of life.

And thou, my friend, my brother, wast thou not seeking also something that thou didst never find? I never read all the secrets of thy soul, but I read therein too many things that resembled mine not to believe that thou, too, wast restless and tormented. Even as mine, thy quest was vain. Our search is bootless. We seek and only find—ourselves. For, to every one of us, the world is only what we have within us. Poor Mitzi, thou hadst not, as had I, a brain with many convolutions, and speech, and complex apparatus, and books rich with the spoils of time to illumine thy path withal. The light of thine eyes is extinguished, and the world with it; that world whereof thou knewest scarcely anything. Oh, if thy beloved little shade could but hear me speak, I would say to it: "A little while and my eyes, too, will close for ever, and I shall have learnt but little more than thou concerning the mystery of Life and Death. As for that Unknown World which I was seeking, rightly did I think when I was a little child that it was close at hand. The Unknown World is all about us; it is everything that is outside us. And, since we can never escape from ourselves, we shall discover it never."

CHAPTER XV

MONSIEUR MÉNAGE

NDER the personal direction of the landlord, M. Bellaguet, our block of flats on the quay was respectable, quiet, and, as the saying goes, "well let." Although he had made a fortune during the Restoration and the July government, M. Bellaguet looked after the letting himself, drew up the leases, managed the repairs with parsimony, and, whenever a suite of rooms fell to be redecorated, a thing that rarely happened, supervised the work in person. You never heard of a dozen yards of wall-paper at fourpence the piece being hung anywhere in the building, without the landlord's being there to see it done. For the rest, he was kindly, affable and anxious to oblige his tenants, provided always it didn't cost him money. He dwelt among us as a father among his children, and I used to see his bright blue bedroom curtains from my window. He was not thought any the less of for keeping a close eye on his property. Possibly people esteemed him the more for it, for what entitles wealthy people to consideration is their wealth. Their stinginess, by making them richer, increases

the estimation in which they are held; whereas, if they are generous, they diminish their stock of wealth, and, with it, their credit and reputation.

When M. Bellaguet was a young man, at the time of the Revolution, he had pursued all sorts of avocations. Like his King, he was something of an apothecary. In urgent cases of injury or suffocation, he administered first aid to the sufferers who, good folk, were duly grateful to him for his services. You couldn't see a finer looking old man, one more venerable or more stately in his bearing. He had no "side." Things were told about him that would have done credit to Napoleon. One night he had opened the front door himself rather than disturb his porter. He was a good father; his two daughters testified, by their merry, contented looks, to the kindness of the paternal treatment. In short, M. Bellaguet enjoyed the unanimous esteem of all who dwelt within his walls, wherever indeed his Turkish cap and flowered dressing gown came within the range of vision. The rest of the world always called him "That old sharper, Bellaguet."

He had attained to that bad eminence by having been mixed up in some case of swindling and corruption which involved the July Government in the thunder and lightning of a first class scandal. M. Bellaguet was jealous of the honour of his establishment, and only "let" to tenants of unblemished reputation. And if the fair Madame Moser was the

only one of them not quite above suspicion, she was
at least vouched for by an ambassador and conducted
herself with perfect propriety. But the house was
very large, and divided up into numerous flats, some
of which were small, low, and dingy. The attics,
which were more numerous than was necessary for
the servants' accommodation, were poky, incon-
venient and draughty; hot in summer and cold in
winter. Very sensibly M. Bellaguet reserved the
small flats, garrets and attics for people like Monsieur and Madame Debas and Madame Petit, the
spectacle-seller; little people who didn't pay much
rent but paid it regularly every quarter.

M. Bellaguet was a handy man and had himself
fitted up a little studio in the loft, where M. Ménage
did his painting. This studio was just opposite
Mélanie's room, from which it was separated by the
width of a narrow, sticky, grimy, spider-haunted
passage, which always smelt of the sink. The stairs
ended there, and were very steep at the top. Right
in front of you as you came up was the door of
Mélanie's room. It was heavily wainscoted and lit
by a skylight of greenish glass which had been broken
in several places and was patched up with paper. The
glass was thick with dust and begrimed the face of
the heavens. Mélanie's bed was covered with a
coloured quilt ornamented with an oft-repeated de-
sign, printed in red, representing a young girl receiv-
ing a prize for good conduct. That, with a walnut

chest of drawers, made up the total of my dear nanny's worldly belongings. Opposite her room was the door of the artist's studio. A visiting card with M. Ménage's name on it was nailed to the door. On the right, facing the door, in the dingy light that trickled through a skylight covered with cobwebs, you could see a sink with its waste pipe, whence there proceeded an everlasting smell of greens. At this end of the passage, facing the quay, it was only about ten paces or so up to the skylight. At the other extremity the only light was a faint glimmer that came up the staircase. The passage disappeared in the gloom and seemed to me to be endless. My imagination peopled it with monsters.

Sometimes my good Mélanie, when she went to put her linen away in her chest of drawers, permitted me to accompany her. But I was not allowed on the top floor alone, and I was expressly forbidden to enter the painter's studio, or even to go near it. According to Mélanie, I should not have been able to bear the sight of it. She herself had been scared out of her wits to see a skeleton hanging there and human limbs pale as death stuck up along the walls. This description awoke fear and curiosity within me, and I was burning with desire to gain entrance to the studio of M. Ménage. One day I had gone up with my old nurse to her attic where she began to fold up numberless old pairs of stockings and I deemed that the favourable moment had arrived. I slipped out of the room and quietly covered the two paces that divided me from the studio. I could see daylight through the keyhole and was just going to put my eye to it when, terror-stricken at the horrible noise the rats were making overhead, I started back and hurriedly retreated into Mélanie's room. This did not prevent my telling her all the things I had seen through the keyhole.

"I saw," I said, "human limbs as pale as death. There were millions of them—it was frightful. I saw skeletons dancing round in a circle, and a monkey blowing a trumpet—it was frightful. I saw seven women. They were very beautiful and wore dresses of gold and silver, and cloaks the same colour as the sun and the moon and the weather. They were hanging with their throats cut, all along the wall, and their blood was flowing in torrents over the white marble floor."

I was thinking what else to say I had seen, when Mélanie asked me, ironically, if I had really seen all those things in so short a time. I expunged the ladies and the skeletons from the indictment; possibly I had not seen them very plainly. But I stuck to it that I had seen "the human limbs as pale as death." And perhaps I really believed I had.

CHAPTER XVI

SHE LAID HER HAND ON MY HEAD

MORIN had a full-blown face and big lips, which, curving upwards at each corner, joined company with a pair of pepper and salt whiskers. His eyes, his nose, his mouth, all his broad, open countenance seemed, literally, to breathe frankness. He was simple in his dress, meticulously clean, and smelt of primrose soap. M. Morin was neither young nor old, and, if he was in the position of the man in the story whose two lady admirers wished to make him match their respective ages, it was certainly Madame Morin, his wife, who pulled out his dark hairs, for she seemed older than he. Her manners also were superior, and she bore herself with much elegance for a woman of her station. But I did not like her because she was sad.

Madame Morin was concierge at a house near ours, which also belonged to M. Bellaguet, and she performed the duties of the porter's lodge with an air of melancholy distinction. Her pale, withered features might well have belonged to the daughter of some illustrious but ill-fated line, and my mother

used to say she was like Queen Marie Amélie. M.
Morin also did his share of work in the porter's box;
but that he looked on as the least of his duties. Two
other important employments occupied the bulk of
his time and energies: he was M. Bellaguet's facto-
tum, and an employé at the Chamber of Deputies.
My father held him in such high esteem that he left
me in his company whole mornings together. M.
Morin was much respected. Everybody in the district knew him, and he had his niche in history because he had carried the Comte de Paris in his arms
on the 24th. February, 1848.

It will be remembered that, after Louis Philippe
had abdicated in favour of his grandson, and the
Royal Family had taken to flight, the Duchesse
d'Orleans, quitting the palace now invaded by the
populace, proceeded in the company of her two children, the Comte de Paris and the Duc de Chartres,
both of tender age, and a few loyal servitors, to the
Chamber of Deputies, where she caused herself to
be announced as mother of the new King, and Queen
Regent of the Realm. Simultaneously with her entry, a group of Republicans burst tumultuously into
the Chamber. Erect at the foot of the tribune,
clasping her two children by the hand, she waited
for the Assembly to ratify her appointment. The
applause that had greeted her entry swiftly died
away. The majority were not in favour of a regency. Sauzet, the President, called on all non-

members to withdraw from the Chamber. With
slow and measured steps the princess made her way
from the hemicycle, but, actuated either by ambition
or a mother's love, she resolved to uphold her sons'
rights, and, reckless of the perils that encompassed
her, refused to leave the Hall. Ascending by the
central stairway to the top of the amphitheatre, she
there unfolded a paper and essayed to address the
assembly. This little woman, so pale in her flowing
widow's weeds, had a power over individual hearts,
but it was not given her to move and to sway multi-
tudes. Her voice was inaudible; you could scarcely
see her amid the shouting groups that surged around
her. Suddenly the dull murmur without grew louder
and nearer. The doors were battered down with
the butt end of rifles, and working men, students,
and National Guards came pouring into the hemicycle shouting:

"Down with the Bourbons! Down with the
King! The Republic for ever!"

Shots were fired off in the corridors. But, above
the shouting and the noise of firearms, there fell
upon the ear a sound, distant, confused, and faint as
yet, but more terrible than all—the billows of the
human ocean beating against the Palace walls. Soon
another wave of men came flooding in, surging this
time round the public tribune, and overwhelming the
assembly. Bands of ruffians armed with pikes, cut-
lasses and pistols, incited each other to slaughter.

Lamartine was in the tribune, and was suspected (quite wrongly) of speaking in favour of a regency. Rifles and blood-stained swords were pointed in his direction. The panic stricken deputies made a rush for the doors. The Duchesse d'Orleans was borne along with her children by the avalanche of fugitives, pushed towards the little door that opens on the left of the office, and swept out into the narrow passage, where, trampled upon and nearly suffocated between the deputies who were trying to get out and the mob who were trying to get in, crushed against the wall, and separated from her children, she fell half fainting at the foot of the staircase. It happened that Morin was just then in the passage and, hearing a child crying, he looked about him and caught sight of the little Comte de Paris, who had been knocked down and was being trampled under foot. He raised him in his arms, carried him through the *salons* and vestibule, and, passing him through a little window that opened on to the garden, handed him over to an artillery officer who was looking for his royal charges.

Meanwhile, the Duchess, who had taken refuge in one of the Presidential *salons*, was calling loudly for her children. They brought her the Comte de Paris, and told her that the Duc de Chartres was safe and sound, disguised as a girl, in one of the Palace attics.

Such was M. Morin's story. He related it fre-

quently and always wound up with the following
reflection:

"All through this trying time the Duchesse
d'Orleans displayed extraordinary courage, and such
powers of resistance as few men would have been
capable of. If only she had been eighteen inches
taller her son would have been king. But she was
too small. You couldn't see her in such a crowd."

The most convincing evidence of the high esteem
in which M. Morin and his wife were held by my
parents was the fact that they allowed me to be with
them as much as I liked, although they were very
particular concerning the people with whom I associated. Their strictness in these matters was a worry
to me. On the floor above us, for example, there
lived a certain Madame Moser, concerning whom a
good deal of whispering went on. She used to spend
long, idle days alone in her rooms, which were furnished in Oriental style; she wore a pink dressing-
gown, slippers of pale blue and gold, and she was
daintily perfumed. Every time an opportunity offered, she carried me off to her rooms to amuse her.
Stretched languorously on the sofa, she would take
me playfully in her arms. I was just going to relate,
in quite good faith, that she hoisted me up in the air
on the sole of her foot, like a toy dog, but I remembered, just in time, that I wasn't pretty enough for
that, and I probably got the notion from Fragonard's
Gimblette, which I saw for the first time when

Madame Moser's pretty feet had for many a year
been resting in the eternal shades; but memories of
divers times have a habit of changing places in the
mind, of dissolving one into another and forming
themselves into a single picture. That is what I am
afraid of in these tales of mine, which if they have
not the merit of truthfulness have no merit at all.
Madame Moser gave me sweets, told me stories
about brigands, and sang me love songs. Unhappily
for me, my parents forbade me to respond to the
advances of this lady, and threatened me with their
direst displeasure if ever I crossed the threshold of
those Oriental rooms with their alluring colours and
insinuating odours. I was also forbidden to venture
up into the attics into M. Ménage's studio. Mélanie announced as a reason for this that M. Ménage
was in the habit of suspending livid pieces of the
human body and skeletons, in his studio. But those
were by no means the only complaints she had to lay
against her neighbour, the painter. She informed
M. Danquin one day that that horrible creature,
Ménage, prevented her sleeping by singing and playing all night long with his friends, so that it was like
Bedlam let loose, and my godfather told the dear
simple creature, whom he was not ashamed to make
fun of, that these artistic people not only sing and
dance the livelong night, but that they quaff blazing
punch from dead men's skulls. Mélanie was much
too proper a person to doubt my godfather's word;

moreover, the painter blackened his reputation in the eyes of this highly respectable old servant by a deed more horrible still.   One night, when she went up to her attic, candle in hand, Mélanie saw on the door of her room a little Cupid sketched in chalk; his bow and his quiver were suspended between his wings, and with a suppliant air he was beating at the closed door with his little fist.   Strongly suspecting that M. Ménage was responsible for this compromising picture, she called him a rogue and a scoundrel, and once more repeated her injunction that I was to have nothing whatever to do with so ill-bred a ruffian.

Few, in fact, were the people who were deemed worthy of close acquaintanceship with me.   I was not allowed to play in the courtyard with the child of M. Bellaguet's cook, young Alphonse, who was bold, and skilled in cunning tricks, for his manners were bad and he said coarse things, made long noses at people, and ran the streets.   One day Alphonse took me to a baker's in the Rue Dauphine, where they sold trimmings from sacramental wafers, of which he ordered a pennyworth, and for which I paid, being the rich one of the party.   We divided it into two portions, which we carried away in our pinafores.   Alphonse, however, ate the whole lot as we were going along.   This escapade got me into a serious scrape, and I was compelled to break with Alphonse.   Nor was I permitted to associate with

Honoré Dumont.   Honoré, whose father was a
High Court Judge, was of good family, and fair as
day, but he was cruel to animals and endowed with
perverted instincts.   I was, however, given full leave
to enjoy the company of Monsieur and Madame
Morin.

I availed myself but sparingly of this permission
with regard to Madame Morin; for, wearing an
elaborate white head-dress, after the manner of
Queen Marie Amélie, her long dismal face yellower
than an orange, she radiated an atmosphere of melancholy and desolation.   Even so, if only Madame
Morin had inspired those who approached her with
a vast and fathomless sadness, a splendid desolation,
a sense of some abysmal calamity, I should have,
perhaps, been conscious of that sort of pleasure
which I experienced from anything excessive, monstrous, or out of the common order, but the melancholy of Madame Morin was regular, moderate,
monotonous, and hum-drum; it soaked into me like
fine rain, and made me feel quite numb.   Madame
Morin rarely quitted her lodge, which had been fitted
up at the side of the carriage entrance.   It was narrow, low and damp, and the only thing about it
worthy of note was the bed, which was so lavishly
furnished with palliasses, mattresses, blankets, coun-
terpanes, bolsters, pillows, and eiderdowns, that it
seemed to me incredible that anyone could sleep in it
without being suffocated.   I suppose that Monsieur

and Madame Morin, who used to sleep in it every
night, owed their miraculous preservation to the
sprig of boxwood which, stuck under the cross of a
china holy water stoup, surmounted the couch of
death.

A wreath of orange blossom under a glass globe
adorned the walnut chest of drawers. On the black
marble chimney-piece, a clock, also covered with a
glass globe, half Gothic and half Turkish in style,
served as a stand for a gilt group representing, as
Madame Morin informed me, "Mathilde plighting
her troth to Malek-Adhel amid the storm in the
desert." I inquired no further, not that I was not
an inquisitive and curious little boy, but because the
story, thus incomplete, charmed me by reason of its
mystery; and the names of Malek-Adhel and Mathilde remain associated in my memory with the
smell of boiled leeks, braised onions, and soot that
clung about Madame Morin's lodge. That worthy
person, wearing her habitual air of melancholy, used
to do her cooking in an oven that was very low. The
flue pipe was fitted into the chimney, and was for
ever smoking. The liveliest amusement I found in
her company was to watch her skimming the soup
and peeling carrots. The great care she took to
remove as little as possible revealed a parsimonious
mind. On the other hand, M. Morin's occupations
entertained me greatly.

When, armed with carpet brushes, feather mops

and brooms, he prepared to introduce into a room
the order and neatness that were dear to him, he
laughed a merry laugh, and opened his mouth from
ear to ear. His big round eyes lit up, his broad
features beamed. There was something of the heroic
about him that seemed to suggest Hercules going
about his domestic labours in Elis. If I had the good
fortune to come upon him at such a moment in his
day's work, I would hang on to his rough hairy hand
all smelling of yellow soap, and we would go up the
stairs together and enter one of the suites of apartments entrusted to his care during the absence of the
owners and their servants. Two of them I remember well.

I can still see in my mind's eye the spacious *salon*
of the Comtesse Michaud, with its mirrors and all
their phantoms, its furniture shrouded in white
covers, and the portrait of a general erect in full
dress uniform amid a whirlwind of smoke and grape-
shot. Morin informed me that the picture represented General Comte Michaud, at Wagram, with
all his decorations. The third floor was more to
my taste. It was the *pied-à-terre* of Comte Colonna
Walewski. A thousand and one strange and charming things were to be seen there. Chinese figures,
silken screens, folding screens in lacquer, narghiles,
Turkish pipes, suits of armour, ostrich eggs, guitars,
Spanish fans, portraits of women, luxurious divans
and heavy curtains. When I expressed the wonder

I felt in the presence of all these strange objects, Morin, with a touch of pride in his manner, would remark that the Comte Walewski was a dashing blade. He had been living for a time in England, and was now passing through Paris on his way to Italy, where he had been appointed ambassador. I got to know the world when I was with Morin.

It happened that one day, as I was mounting with him up the rather narrow staircase that led to the apartments of the Comtesse Michaud, the Comte Walewski and some other tenants whose names I forget, (the outside of the house, which I often look at, has not changed; what reason unknown to myself, what secret instinct has kept me from going to see whether the staircase is still the same as it was when I was a child?) one day, I say, finding myself with Morin between the first and second landing, we looked up and saw a young lady coming down the stairs. Forthwith Morin, who was the last word in politeness and who always instructed me, as occasion demanded, how to behave like a nice little boy, made me stand up with him close to the wall, told me to hold my cap in my hand, and doffed his own. The young lady was wearing a velvet gown and a cashmere shawl with a big palm-leaf pattern. Her dainty, pale face was encased in a coal-scuttle bonnet. She descended the stairs with graceful air. As she passed us, she lowered her dark bright eyes upon me, and from her little mouth, her tiny little mouth like to a pomegranate, there stole a grave soft voice, the like of which for richness and expression I have never heard in another.

"Morin," she said, "is this your little boy? He is a nice little fellow." And she laid her white-gloved hand on my head.

Morin having informed her that I belonged to one of the neighbours, she went on:

"Yes, he's a nice little boy; but his parents ought to be careful. He looks very delicate, and his cheeks are flushed."

Those eyes, which looked on me so gently, lit up on the stage with the "dark flame" wherewith Phedra was consumed. That slender hand, laid affectionately on my head, used to thrill the audience as it gave the signal for the murder of Pyrrhus. Rachel, already stricken with the disease which was to bring her to the grave, was seeking out the signs of it upon the face of a poor little boy whom she chanced to encounter on the staircase with the porter. I was not old enough to go to the theatre until she had given up the stage, and I never saw her perform, but I can still feel her little gloved hand on my head.

CHAPTER XVII

"A BROTHER IS A FRIEND BESTOWED ON US BY NATURE"

Y Aunt Chausson lived at Angers. She had been born and married there. Having been left a widow, she eked out her slender means with the strictest regard to economy and used to make a little sparkling wine, of which sne was very proud and very niggardly. Whenever she came to Paris, which was looked upon as a long journey in those days, she stayed with my parents. The announcement of her coming used to be received without enthusiasm by my mother, and also by old Mélanie, who was afraid of her stingy, provincial ways.

"It's a funny thing," my father used to say, "but my sister Renée, although she was married for eight years before she lost her husband, exhibits the type of old maidishness in all its baleful perfection."

My Aunt Chausson, who was much older than her brother, thin, and parchment-skinned, her clothes skimpy and out of date, appeared a great deal older than she really was, and I looked on her as bowed down with years without respecting her any the more

for that. That is a confession that costs me but little.
Respect for old age does not come naturally to children: it is the result of education and never takes
ᵃa deep hold on them. I did not love my Aunt Chausson, but, having no desire to love her, I felt quite
at my ease in her company. Her arrival caused
me the greatest joy because it necessitated changes
in the house, and I delighted in any kind of change.
My bed was wheeled into the little rose-flowered
sitting-room, and I was in the seventh heaven.

The third time she came to stay with us after I
was born, she examined me with greater attention
than on any previous occasion, and the examination
was not favourable. She discovered defects that
were both numerous and contradictory: an importunate turbulence which she blamed my mother for not
sternly correcting, a quickness unnatural to my age,
which in her view boded nothing good. I was in-
curably lazy, immoderately restless, dull and back-
ward, far too precocious. To these various and unfavourable qualities, she assigned a common origin.
According to my aunt, the whole evil (and it was a
big one) arose from the fact that I was an only boy.

When my mother was worried because I was pale
and languid, my aunt would say:

"How can you expect him to be bright and healthy
when he has no child to play with, no little brother?"

If I didn't know my multiplication table, if I upset the ink down my velvet tunic, if I ate too many

biscuits or dried apples, if I obstinately refused to re-
cite "The Beasts that died of the Plague" to
Madame Caumont, if I fell down and raised a bump
on my forehead, if Sultan Mahmud scratched me,
if I wept over my canary which was found one day
motionless in its cage, with its eyes closed and its
feet in the air, if the rain came down or the wind
howled, it was all because I hadn't a brother. One
evening at the dinner table I took it into my head
to put a pinch of pepper on a piece of cream tart
that was being reserved for Mélanie, who delighted
in sweet things. My mother caught me in the act
and reproached me for an action which she did not
consider a credit either to my intelligence or to my
feelings. My Aunt Chausson, who dotted the i's and
crossed the t's of this verdict, and read in this act of
mischief the symptoms of a deep-seated depravity,
excused me on the ground that I had no brother or
sister.

"He lives alone. Solitude is not a good thing. It
develops the perverse instincts, the seeds of which
are already in the child. He is unbearable. Not
only does he try to put poison in this old servant's
pudding, but he blows down the back of my neck,
and hides my spectacles. If I lived here long, Antoinette my dear, the boy would drive me crazy."

As I felt perfectly innocent of trying to poison
anybody, and I should not have had the least compunction in driving Aunt Chausson crazy, I was not

much affected by her accusations. So far from taking what the old lady said for gospel I was much inclined to go counter to her opinions, and if she said she wished I had a brother or a sister it was quite enough for me to hope that I should never have either one or the other. Moreover, I got on quite well without a playmate. I may not have found the time pass so quickly as it does to-day, but I never found it heavy on my hands, because, even then, my inner life was very active, I felt and pondered things deeply and absorbed everything in the external world which I could take in with my childish intelligence. Furthermore, I knew that little brothers, when they come, are usually quite tiny, knowing not how to walk, incapable of conversation and offering no sort of usefulness. There was no certainty that, when mine was grown big, I should love him or be loved by him. The august and familiar example of Cain and Abel did not tend to reassure me.

It is true that from my windows I used to see the twin pumpkins, Alfred and Clément Caumont, slumbering side by side in a sort of deep vegetable peace. But then I often saw Jean, the bricklayer's apprentice, punching into his brother Alphonse like so much mortar, while Alphonse replied by putting out his tongue and making long noses at him.

So that it seemed to me rather a difficult thing to base one's views on any authoritative example. And, in point of fact, being an only child presented, in

my opinion, distinct advantages, among others those
of never being thwarted, of not being obliged to
share my parents' love with others, and of safeguard-
ing that taste, that necessity, for communing with
myself which I had always experienced from my
earliest childhood.   At the same time I wanted to
have a little brother so that I could love him; for
my mind was full of uncertainties and contradictions.

One day I asked my dear mamma to tell me in confidence whether she didn't think she would give me a
little brother.   Laughingly she said "No," adding
that she was too much afraid he might turn out to be
another naughty little boy like me.   This did not
seem to me to be taking the matter seriously.   My
Aunt Chausson went back to Angers, and I thought
no more about the subject that had occupied my mind
so deeply during her stay with us.   But some days
after her departure, some days or some months (for
what gives me the greatest trouble in these narra-
tives, is the matter of chronology) my godfather, M.
Danquin came one morning to have lunch with us.   It
was a brilliant day.   The sparrows were twittering
on the housetops.   Suddenly I was seized with an irresistible desire to do something out of the ordinary,
something that should, if possible, partake of the
nature of the miraculous, in order to vary the monotony of things.   The means at my disposal for the
arrangement and execution of such an enterprise
were very meagre.   Having an idea that I might find

something to my hand in the kitchen, I entered and
found it glowing, fragrant and untenanted. Just as
she was going to dish up, Mélanie, in her usual fashion, had gone off to the grocer's or the fruiterer's for
some herb or grain or condiment she had forgotten.
On the stove stood a sizzling *casserole* of jugged
hare. At the sight of it, I was seized with a sudden
inspiration. In obedience to its dictàtes, I took the
jugged hare off the fire and went and hid it in the
cupboard where the brooms were kept. This move
was successfully carried out save that four fingers of
my right hand and both my knees were burnt, my
face scorched, my pinafore, my stockings, and my
shoes entirely spoilt, and that three parts of the
sauce, with some pieces of bacon and a lot of little
onions, were upset all over the floor. Incontinent I
rushed away to fetch the Noah's Ark I had had given
me for Christmas, and poured all the animals it contained into a magnificent copper saucepan which I
put on the stove in place of the hare. This fricas-
see very pleasantly recalled to my mind what I had
learnt, from hearsay and from picture books, of the
feast of Gargantua. For, if the giant spitted with
his two pronged fork whole oxen at a time, here
was I compounding a dish of all the animals in creation, from the elephant and the giraffe down to the
butterfly and the grasshopper. I revelled in anticipa-
tion over the amazement that would be Mélanie's
when she, good, simple soul, thinking to find the hare

which she had prepared, discovered in its stead, the
lion and the lioness, the he-ass and the she-ass, the
elephant and his lady—in a word all the animals that
had been saved from the Flood, not omitting Noah
and his family whom I had stewed up with the rest
by inadvertence. But the thing did not turn out as
I had hoped. A most intolerable stench proceeding
from the kitchen, a stench unprovided for by me, and
stupefying to the others, began to invade every room
in the place. My mother, coughing and choking,
came running to the kitchen to find out what had happened, and there discovered poor old Mélanie, gasp-
ing for breath, with her basket still on her arm, just
taking hold of the saucepan in which the charred remains of the occupants of the Ark were smouldering
hideously.

"My 'castrole,' my lovely 'castrole'!" cried Mélanie, in accents of despair.

I had come to triumph over the success of my plot;
I remained to feel the crushing weight of shame and
remorse. And it was in quavering tones that, at
Mélanie's summons, I revealed that the jugged hare
was to be found in the broom cupboard.

I was not scolded. My father, paler than usual,
pretended not to see me. My mother's cheeks were
very flushed, and she looked at me askance, scanning
my face to see whether she could detect the symptoms
of incipient crime or madness. But the most deplor-
able spectacle of all was presented by my godfather.

The corners of his mouth, usually framed so jovially within a pair of round cheeks and a fat chin, drooped most ruefully. Behind his gold-rimmed spectacles, his eyes, so lately beaming, had ceased to twinkle.

When Mélanie brought in the hare, her eyes were red and tears were streaming down her cheeks. I could bear it no longer, and, getting up from the table, I rushed to my poor old friend, hugged her with all my might, and burst into a flood of tears.

From the pocket of her apron she drew her chequered handkerchief, gently wiped my eyes with her knotted hand all smelling of parsley, and said in a voice broken with sobs:

"Don't cry, Master Pierre, don't cry!"

Turning to my mother, my godfather said:

"Pierrot is not really a bad boy at heart; but he's an only child. He is lonely and doesn't know what to do with himself. Put him to boarding-school. He will be under a healthy discipline, and will have little friends to play with."

On hearing these words, I remembered the advice which Aunt Chausson had given my mamma, and I longed for a little brother so that I might not be sent to a boarding-school, and also that I might love and be loved by him.

I knew that a brother is a gift bestowed by Nature, and, without being aware of the conditions on which the gift is vouchsafed to families in favour with the heavenly powers, I was certain that, to produce it, nothing could replace that force which causes the seed to germinate and life to flourish on the earth. I had an obscure yet profound intuition of the mysterious power which nourished me after having brought me into the world, and I was perfectly well able to differentiate the works of Cybele, whom I adored though I knew not her name, from the most marvellous of man's productions. It would have caused me no difficulty to believe that a magician might fashion a man capable of walking, speaking and eating, but I could never have persuaded myself that such a man was of the same substance as a man produced by Nature. In a word, I abandoned the idea of ever having a brother according to the flesh, and resolved that adoption should obtain what Nature denied me.

To be sure, I did not know that the Emperor Hadrian by adopting Antoninus Pius, and Antoninus by adopting Marcus Aurelius, had given the world forty-two years of tranquil happiness. Of that I had no idea, but, nevertheless, it seemed to me that adoption was an excellent practice. I did not regard it from the strictly legal point of view, for of jurisprudence I was completely ignorant. At the same time I looked upon it as a process invested with a certain solemnity. That was rather to my taste, and I had a vague notion that my parents would put on their best clothes to receive the child that I should present to them for adoption. The difficulty was to find him.

My field of research was very limited; I saw few
people, and none of the families I visited would have
consented to hand over one of their children, without
some powerful motive, such a motive, for example,
as compelled the mother of Moses to expose her little baby on the banks of the Nile. Certainly Madame Caumont would never have agreed to part
with either of her pumpkins. It occurred to me that
it might be less difficult to obtain a little workhouse
child and I broached the subject to my friend Morin,
who scratched his head and said that to take a foun-
dling into one's family was a very risky business, and
that, moreover, my parents could not adopt a child
because they had one already. Knowing nothing of
the law, I was quite unimpressed by that argument,
and, in the course of the walks I took with Mélanie,
in the Luxembourg, the Tuileries, and the Jardin des
Plantes, I continued to look out for a brother to
adopt. Despite poor old Mélanie's injunctions to
the contrary, I went and tried to make friends with
all the little boys we used to meet. I was shy, awkward, and delicate-looking, and generally got nothing but taunts and contumely for my pains. Or, if
by any chance I discovered a child as shy as I was
myself, we parted from each other without a word,
with drooping heads and full hearts, neither being
able to make known to the other the affection that
stirred within him. The conviction was borne in
upon me at that time that, though not perfect, I was

more worthy than the majority of other folk.

Some little time after that, one autumn day when I was alone in the drawing-room, I saw a little Savoyard, as black as an imp, come stepping out from the chimney. The apparition was not so alarming as diverting.

Little Savoyards, who, like that one, did chimney sweeping, were in those days not uncommon in Paris. In old houses, such as ours, the flues are as wide as the walls are thick, quite big enough for a child to climb up them, and as a rule the work was performed by little boys from Savoy. It used to be said that they learnt how to climb from watching their monkeys, but they used to have a rope with knots in it to help them. The youngster of my story, all besmeared with soot, with a little brewer's cap pulled right down to his ears, displayed, when he smiled, a set of dazzling white teeth and a pair of bright red lips, which he licked to clean away the dirt. On his shoulders he carried a coil of rope and a trowel, and he looked a little shrimp of a thing in his vest and shorts. I liked the look of him, and asked his name. He answered in nasal but very gentle tones that he was called Adéodat, and that he came from Gervex near Bonneville.

I went up to him, and, with an affectionate gesture, said:

"Will you be my brother?"

He rolled a pair of wondering eyes within his

black and white harlequin's mask, opened his mouth
from ear to ear, and nodded his head in assent.

Thereupon, in a sort of frenzy of fraternal affection, I told him to wait a moment, and rushed
away to the kitchen. Ransacking larder, cupboard,
and pantry, I lighted upon a cheese, of which I forthwith took possession. It was one of those cheeses
which they make at Neufchâtel, and which, being
shaped like the wooden plugs they stick into the bung
holes (*bonde*) of wine casks, have come by the
name of *bondon*. This one was in perfect condition,
with little red flecks showing here and there on its
bluish, velvety surface. I brought it back to my
brother, who had remained as stock still as if he had
been a clock. He rolled a pair of astonished eyes,
and accepted it with alacrity. He drew his knife
from his pocket, began to dig into the *bondon*, and
conveyed large pieces of it to his mouth on the point
of the blade. He moved his jaws with a grave,
meditative deliberation that was doubtless habitual
with him, never pausing a second to take breath. At
this point my mother came on the scene. Little then
remained of the bondon but the skin. I thought it
incumbent on me to explain:

"Mamma, this is my brother. I have adopted
him."

"That is very nice," said my mother smiling. "But
he will choke himself. Give him something to
drink."

Mélanie, whom by good luck I found in the kitchen, brought in a glass of water coloured with a
little wine. My brother drank it down at a gulp,
wiped his mouth on his sleeve and heaved a sigh of
content.

My mother asked him about his home, his family,
and his circumstances, and he must have answered
becomingly, for, when he had gone, my mamma
said:

"He's a nice little boy, that brother of yours."

She decided that his master, who lived in the
Rue des Boulangers, should be asked to let him come
to us one Sunday.

I must confess that Adéodat, when washed and in
his best clothes, pleased me less than when wearing
his black brewer's cap and his mask of soot. He
had his lunch in the kitchen, where we went to look
at him, my mother and I, feeling a little compunction
at our curiosity. Old Mélanie signed to us not to
come too near for fear of vermin. He behaved with
perfect politeness, but he refused point blank to fall
to until he had put on his hat, which had been hung
up on a peg. Such manners we thought a little rustic. When one comes to think of it, however, they
were in reality very aristocratic. In the seventeenth
century a man of quality never sat down to table
with his head uncovered. It was seemly that he
should wear his hat during a meal, since etiquette
compelled him to be continually taking it off; when,

for example, he received an attention from his neighbour, or when he bestowed his services on the lady
at his side. In his new "Treatise on polite observances practised in France," published in Paris in the
year 1702, M. Courtin under the heading "Behaviour at the table," expressly states as follows: "If
a person of rank proposes a health, or drinks to your
own, you must remove your hat, bending forward a
little over the table, until he has drunk. When he
speaks to you, you must uncover before replying,
taking care not to have your mouth full. The same
civility should be observed whenever he addresses
you until he requests you to desist, after which you
should remain covered, lest you should weary him
with excessive ceremony." Adéodat wore his hat
during the repast like an old time courtier of the
days of Louis XIV; but, truth to tell, he did not
doff it so often. He put the meat on his bread and
conveyed the pieces to his mouth with his knife, and
he was very grave. After luncheon, at my mother's
request, he sang to us, in a voice scarcely audible, a
folk song of his native country:

> "Escouto, Jeannetto,
> Veux-tu d'biaux habits?
> La ridetto."

He replied briefly, and very sensibly, to my dear
mamma's questions. We learnt that he worked in
Paris during the winter and, when the spring
began to draw near, returned on foot to his own

country. His mother, being too poor to buy a cow, worked for hire in the creameries. He worked with her or went gathering myrtle berries or *"maurels"* as he called them, on the mountain side. They lived on pancakes and did not get too much of them.

I determined to save up and buy a cow for Adéodat's mother, but I soon forgot all about it. The little chimney-sweep went home when the spring came. Mamma sent some woollen garments and a little money to his mother. And believing him to be a steady and intelligent boy she wrote asking the village schoolmaster to teach him the three "R's" saying that she would pay the expense. Adéodat wrote a letter in printed characters to thank her.

I often inquired for my brother. I asked for him again as the winter came on.

"Your brother is staying in his own country," answered my mother, fearing lest she should grieve me by saying more.

My brother Adéodat was never destined to come back again. He lay sleeping in the little cemetery of his native village. My mother had heard about him from the schoolmaster at Gervex, but she never showed me the letter. It informed her that little Adéodat had died of meningitis without ever knowing how ill he was, only wondering to find his head so heavy. A few hours before he died he spoke of the kind Madame Nozière and sang his song:

"Escouto, Jeannetto . . ."

CHAPTER XVIII

NE morning, having accompanied old Mélanie into her attic, I examined with greater attention than usual the coloured quilt which she had on her bed and which, as I have already mentioned, was ornamented with a design representing a village school treat. The subject was printed in red and many times repeated. It seemed to me to have a grace about it. It appealed to my imagination and excited my curiosity. Mélanie upbraided me for wasting my time on silly things.

"What can you find to admire in that old thing, Pierrot? It's been patched over and over again. Madame Sainte-Lucie, where I was in service, had it all spick and span on her death-bed, and I got it when the young gentlemen shared out their mother's wardrobe among the servants."

Still I went on plying her with questions.

"Who is that pretty young lady the gentleman is crowning with roses? Why these drums and trumpets, these maidens all in a row, these peasants hand in hand?"

"Where do you see all that, mon petit monsieur?

143

You can't possibly see all those things there. I must put on my glasses and look."

She perceived that I had invented nothing.

"Upon my word, it is so, sure enough. They're all in the picture, young maidens, gentlemen, countryfolk, and goodness knows what besides. Well, I never! I've had that quilt on my bed fifty years and I never noticed those things. Why, if anybody had asked me what colour it was I shouldn't have been able to tell them. And I've darned it often enough too!"

As I was coming out of the room with Mélanie I heard a noise of crutches and footsteps tapping along at the dark end of the corridor, and slowly getting nearer. I stopped, and was frightened out of my life when I saw, slowly emerging from the shadow, a hideous old hag, bent double, her back where her head ought to be, and a cavernous looking countenance on her chest, her right eye covered up with an enormous green shade. I seized hold of Mélanie's apron. When the apparition had gone by, she told me it was old Mother Cochelet. Mélanie could tell me nothing about her, never speaking with her, or, indeed, with anyone, an assertion which my aged friend often repeated but which must not be interpreted according to the strict meaning of the word, but which should be taken rather in the light of a testimony rendered by herself to her own discretion. Old Mother Cochelet lived in a noisome hovel at the far end of the passage. However, she was not believed to be in want because she had three cats for which she bought a pennyworth of lights every morning. M. Bellaguet had frequently offered to get her into an almshouse, but she refused with such energy that he had to give up the idea.

"She is proud," said Mélanie. Then lowering her voice, she added: "Elle est pour le roi" (Mélanie pronounced it *roué*). "She is for the King." Folk say that up in her garret, where everything is rotting away, she has a magnificent counterpane embroidered with fleurs de lis.

That was all I got to know about Mother Cochelet. But some time later on, when we were taking our walk in the Tuileries, Mélanie and I, we came across the old woman, who was sitting on one of the seats and offering a pinch of snuff to an old military pensioner. She was wearing a shabby black straw hat over her fluted cap, in the 1820 manner, and had a dirty old yellow shawl wrapped round her shoulders. Her chin, resting on her crutch, was shaking, and the shade over her eye was trembling.

The pensioner's nose and chin were like a pair of nut-crackers. They were talking together.

"Let's go and sit somewhere else," said Mélanie. And she got up. But anxious to hear what Mother Cochelet was saying, I went close up to the seat where she was sitting. She wasn't talking, she was singing. She was singing, or rather she was humming:

"Que ne suis-je la fougère?"

CHAPTER XIX

MADAME LAROQUE AND THE SIEGE OF GRANVILLE

ADAME LAROQUE had apartments in the same house as ourselves, but at the far end of the court, and there she lived with her daughter, Thérèse and her parrot, Navarino. I used to catch sight of her from my window, and sometimes from my bed. Her face was hale, and puckered like the skin of apples that have been stored in a cellar for the winter. She used to appear to me at her nasturtium-bordered window, betwixt a pot of carnations and the pagoda-shaped parrot's cage, looking like one of those worthy housewives the old Flemish masters used to portray in an embrasure of masonry and flowers. Every Saturday, after dinner, which in those days was over about six o'clock, my mother put on her hat to go across the courtyard, and took me with her to spend the evening with the Laroque ladies. She took her work in a bag, so that she might do her sewing or embroidery with her neighbours. The other ladies who visited there did the same. It was a survival of the old regime by no means peculiar to the middle

and lower-middle classes, as one might think to-day. It was, indeed, a custom observed in the time of Louis XVI, by the highest aristocracy, who were, nevertheless, far from being wedded to the simple life. In the reign of Louis XVI, women of the highest rank used to do their sewing together. Madame Vigée-Lebrun relates in her memoirs that, during the period of the Royalist emigration, she was received in Vienna by the Comtesse de Thoun, and that, when there, she used to take her place at the large table round which the princesses of the court worked at their tapestry frames. These remarks of mine are not intended to convey the impression that my dear mamma and I went once a week to call on princesses.

Madame Laroque was an old lady of very simple habits, but in diligence, in patience, and in qualities of the heart she was among the great, and she was endowed with a wisdom in domestic affairs that never failed her in good or evil fortune. She bore within her the experiences of well nigh a century of French national life and of two regimes, the old and the new, united and welded by the hearts and minds of the women who, like her, threw themselves, after the manner of David's Sabine Women, between the contending parties.

Rich and comely, descended from Normandy yeomen of Republican sentiments, Marie Rauline was of marriageable age when the wars of Vendée broke out. When I knew her, she was over eighty, and as she sat in her easy chair, knitting stockings, she used to tell stories of her young days. Her friends had given up listening to them because she told them every day and sometimes, if she had the opportunity, several times a day. Such was the tale of the young suitor, who being no taller than a jack boot, had been rejected as unfit for military service, and, since the Republic would have none of him, Marie Rauline would have none of him either. She used generally to finish off the story by singing the pretty air:

> "Il était un petit homme
> Qui s'appelait Guilleri
> Carabi."

The story Madame Laroque was most fond of telling and the one I delighted most to hear was the story of the siege of Granville.

Marie Rauline married in the year IV a soldier of the Republic, named Eugène Laroque, who subsequently became a captain in the Imperial army. He took part in the Spanish campaign, and being ambushed by some of the irregular troops of Julian Sanchez perished by the hand of an assassin. Left a widow with two daughters, Madame Laroque lived in Paris on the proceeds of a little drapery business. Her elder daughter took the veil and became Superior of the Dames du Saint-Sang at Crecy; she was known as Mother Séraphine. The other made a small fortune as a dressmaker. When I knew them they were already advanced in years. Mother Séraphine, whom I saw but seldom, impressed me by the noble simplicity of her bearing. Mademoiselle Thérèse, her younger sister, I liked for her merry and equable disposition. She was a great hand at making *bêtises*. Now *bêtises* was the name people gave in those days to caramels served in little paper wrappers, a thing I used to look upon as a triumph of art. She was also a very good pianist.

Whenever we went to visit the Laroques, we were always sure to find Mademoiselle Julie, who believed in ghosts and whose friendship I cultivated despite the fact that she was a withered, crabbed creature. But she told ghost stories, and spoke of dire and dreadful things to come, of unheard-of marvels. And, ever since I was five years old, my faith in evil spirits has needed a good deal of bolstering up.

Alas, I found a snake in the grass at Mesdames Laroques', and that was Mademoiselle Alphonsine Dusuel, who, in days gone by, had been wont to stick pins into my legs, what time she hailed me as her "treasure." I still used to complain to my mother about the horrible cruelties perpetrated by Alphonsine, but, in reality, I was more frightened than hurt, or rather, to tell the whole truth, I was really neither hurt nor frightened. She didn't so much as notice my presence now. Alphonsine was fast growing up into a young lady; the perfidies that she perpetrated now

were less simple in their nature, and had other objects in view than a little boy like me. I saw well
enough that she liked to practise her wiles on a
nephew of Mademoiselle Thérèse. His name was
Fulgence Rauline; he played the violin and was going to attend classes at the Conservatoire. Although
I was not jealous by nature, and although Alphonsine was plain and her face all over freckles, I would
still have preferred her to go on sticking pins into
my legs. No, I wasn't jealous and, if I had been,
it would not have been about one of Alphonsine's
favourites; but, being wrapped up in myself and
eager for attention and love, I wanteɑ the whole
world to concern itself with me, even though it were
but to torment me. At the age of five 1 had not
succeeded in getting rid of the old Adam.

When the ladies, old or young, had grown tired of
sewing and folded up their work, we played the game
of Goose, or Loto. I didn't like Loto at all. I am
not saying that I could form any intelligent estimate
of the dismal stupidity of the thing, but it is a fact
that it did not satisfy my young ideas; the thing was
all figures and symbols; it did not appeal to my imagination. My partners also must have found it too
abstract for their taste, since they employed all manner of things to liven it up; not invented out of their
own heads certainly, but handed down from their
forbears. They likened the Arabic symbols, for example, to some tangible object; the figure 7 was a

shovel, 8 was a pumpkin, 11 a pair of legs, 22 a
couple of chicken, 33, two hunchbacks, or else they
would embellish the cold statement of the number
with some poetic tag. Then there were some very
old names given to the numbers, which only Madame
Laroque knew perfectly, such as "1, a hair of Mat-
thew's head," "2, the Testaments Old and New;"
doubtless these additions relieved the game of some
of its monotony, but, all the same, I found it too
abstract for my taste. The noble game of Goose
which was in vogue among the ancient Greeks delighted me beyond measure. In it everything lives
and speaks, it is Nature and Destiny themselves,
it is as marvellous as it is true, and as orderly as it is
hazardous. The prophetic geese stationed at every
"nine" seemed to me like divine beings and, as in
those days I was prone to adore animals, these great
white birds filled me with awe. Their rôle was that
of mystery, all the rest belonged to the domain of
reason. When I was held up at the hostelry, I could
smell the meat roasting. I fell into the well on the
edge of which, for my salvation or my ruin, stood
a pretty peasant girl with crimson stomacher and
white apron. I lost myself in the maze, where it
caused me no surprise to find a Chinese kiosk, such
was my ignorance of Cretan art. I fell off the bridge
into the river. I was flung into prison. I escaped
death by a hair's breadth, and at last I won my way
to the wood guarded by the Heavenly Goose, the

dispenser of all felicity. Sometimes, however, having had my fill of adventures, like Sinbad the Sailor, I gave up tempting Providence. I dared not approach the well or the bridge, the labyrinth or the prison; I went and sat me down on a little red stool at Madame Laroque's feet, and there, well away from the table and the lamp, I got her to tell me the story of the siege of Granville.

And Madame Laroque, as she knitted a stocking, told me the story which I here reproduce word for word:

"On leaving Fougères, M. de la Rochejacquelin, who was in command of the brigands, was for going to Rennes, but some *émigrés,* disguised as peasants, came to him with letters and gold from England, concealed in hollow sticks. Thereupon, M. Henri, as they used to call him among themselves, commanded the brigands to proceed to Granville, because these gentry had a promise from the English to send ships of war to attack the town from the sea, while the brigands attacked it on land. But no reliance ought to be placed on the promises of the English. I heard the same thing said later on by a man from Bressuire. These are things I heard with my own ears and saw with my own eyes. The brigands arrived in their thousands at Granville. They came in such numbers that you could see them from the promenade swarming like ants over the foreshore. The General commanding in the town

marched out to meet them with the volunteers from
the Manche, and the Paris gunners, who wore caps
of liberty tattooed in blue on their arms, with the
words 'Liberty or Death.'   But the number of brigands kept on increasing; they stretched as far as
the eye could see, and M. Henri, who looked like
a young girl, bore himself gallantly as their com-
mander.   Then the General realized that they were
too many for him.   His name was Peyre.   There
were good and bad reports going about concerning him, as there were concerning every one who
was in the public eye in those days.   All the same he
was a straightforward man, and commanded considerable resources.

"That day, my mother being ill in bed, I went to
the Town Hall with our old linen, which had been
requisitioned by the authorities.   The guns were
rumbling and a thick smoke hung over the outlying
parts of the town.   Men were going about shouting, 'We are betrayed, they are coming; every man
for himself.'   The women were shrieking loud
enough to wake the dead.   Then citizen Desmaisons
rushed on to the promenade wearing his plumed
hat and his tricolour scarf and I saw him, quite close
to me, reel like a drunken man, clutch at his breast
and fall face forwards.   He had had a bullet through
the heart.   And, despite the terror I was in, I remember thinking that dying was a pretty quick business.   People were not taking any precautions at

the time and two women had just fallen on the promenade. I managed to reach home by sidling along close up to the wall and found a Paris gunner at the door. He had come to ask for some wood in order to make the cannon balls red hot. 'It's warm,' said he. He was joking, because it was blowing a gale and you could feel the sting of the coming winter.

"I said to him, 'Come and take some wood.' Thereupon the Chappedelaine girl comes rushing up and says, 'Don't you give him my wood, Marie. Isn't the place burning quite enough as it is? Haven't there been enough Christians roasted like swine? You can smell them from here. If you give him wood you'll get what you deserve; when the Vendeans get in they'll put you to death.' It was fear that made her say these things, for there were well-to-do people in the town who were paying money to get the brigands in. 'Mathilde,' said I, 'you can take my word for it that, if these gentry take the town they will restore the toll and bring in the English. However, if you want to go on being a slave and to become an Englishwoman yourself, that's your look out. I'm going to remain free and a Frenchwoman. Long live the Republic!' Then the Parisian tried to kiss me, but I slapped his face, for the look of the thing. Meanwhile people began shouting, 'Look, they're getting ready to storm.' I was afraid, and still more curious than afraid. I slipped down to the promenade and saw the Vendeans thrusting their bayonets into the walls to make themselves a foothold. But the Republicans were firing on them from the top of the ramparts and bringing down the luckless assailants who crashed down on the rocks beneath. At last, seeing the tide was out and that it was no use waiting for the English to come and help them, they took to flight, flinging away their sabots. The shore was strewn with corpses still clasping their beads in their rigid fingers. The Chappedelaine girl shook her fist at them and said they had died too comfortably. And then all the people who had been for surrendering the town began to vilify them for fear they should be denounced as traitors to the Republic."

Thus spake Madame Laroque, and this story of an event that happened more than a hundred and twenty years ago now, I heard from the lips of an eye-witness.

CHAPTER XX

" 'Twas thus those monsters fell did grind their teeth."
—*Ronsard.*

HEY were dreary times at home just then. My father was worried, my mother agitated, and old Mélanie inclined to weep. The chilly silence that reigned at meals was broken only by the briefest of utterances.

"Has Gomboust paid up?"

"Gomboust did not put in an appearance."

"Did you see the bailiff?"

"Rampon has advanced the money, but the interest he wants, good heavens! The man's a regular vampire!"

Then silence again. Their faces were mournful. Joy being as necessary to me as sunlight to plants, I drooped and languished in this atmosphere of gloom.

They were dreary days. My father, who of all men in the world had the least aptitude for business, had gone and mixed himself up in some speculation or other. Why he did so I don't know; blind confidence in a friend, perhaps, or because he wanted to go out of his way to oblige, or because he thought he saw a way of keeping his wife in ease and comfort and providing handsomely for his son's education, or for some philanthropic reason, or, good Lord! it may have been pure wool-gathering and absence of mind. Anyhow, he had joined his friend Gomboust in a scheme to exploit the springs at Saint Firmin, which had been analysed by various eminent chemists and had been recognized by several members of the medical profession as possessing valuable curative properties in disorders of the stomach, liver, and kidneys.

This venture, which was to bring in enormous profits, promptly went smash. It would be quite impossible for me to define the nature of the company that was formed to exploit this mineral water, or to indicate the share of it that was allotted to my father. That were a task for Balzac, not for Pierrot. I readily confine my account of the matter to the impressions left of it on my childish brain.

Adélestan Gomboust, who was the proprietor of the Saint Firmin Springs in the Hautes-Pyrénées, was the owner of a tall paralytic body which gave, so to speak, no sign of life. Lids that never moved covered his hollow eyes. Between his shrunken lips you could just discern the gleam of a couple of white teeth. His face was like a dead man's, but from his mummy-like mouth there issued a voice of delicious clearness, which, like a silver flute, produced modulations of sweetest sound. As he came along guided by a child, and leaning upon crutches, there was something uncanny in his appearance that sent a chill through one's marrow.

"Here's bad luck come our way," sighed Mélanie, as she saw him, and whether it was that she could not remember his name or whether she thought the name an unlucky one, she never uttered it, but always announced him with bated breath as "The gentleman with the skin eyes."

I often used to find myself alone in the drawing-room with this inanimate body. It frightened me, and I hardly dared to look at it.. But no sooner did it open its mouth than the charm began to work. Gomboust taught me how to rig a boat, fly a kite, and make a Hero's fountain. The music of his voice, the orderly sequence of his thoughts, gave me the utmost delight, however little I may have been able to appreciate the art of good speaking. With his expressionless face and his motionless body the man was the very personification of persuasiveness. I was trying to think just now how it was my father, who was so prudent, and so indifferent to money-getting, came to get mixed up in the Saint-Firmin Company. The reason however is evident; he had hearkened to the voice of Gomboust. Gomboust's utterances had the same effect on my parents as they had on me, and this is a proof of it:

It was, I remember, one evening, one of the darkest of those dismal times. M. Paulin, a solicitor, a suave man, M. Bourisse a chamber counsel who

was suäver than M. Paulin, M. Philipeaux, who was
suäver than M. Bourisse, M. Rampon, who advanced,
money on weekly loans, and was suäver than M.
Philipeaux, had all suävely acted on my father's
artless and timid mind till they had thoroughly and
completely frightened him.   My mother, who beheld in Gomboust the arch-contriver of our ruin,
being informed by Mélanie that "the man with
the skin eyes" wished to see her, gave him a very
chilly reception in the lobby, where I was hiding underneath a form pretending that it was the cave of
the nymph Eucharis, and that I was Telemachus. I
lay low and listened to my mother as she heaped reproaches on the head of the motionless Gomboust.
I felt, as it were, a blow at the heart when she said
to him: "Monsieur, you have deceived us; you are
not an honest man."

After a prolonged silence, Gomboust made reply.
His voice trembled and emotion made it even more
musical than usual. I did not understand what he
said. He spoke at great length. My mother listened to him without interrupting. From the place
where I lay concealed I watched her face grow
calmer and her expression soften. She was under
the spell. At luncheon next day my father showed
her a paper which she glanced through, and handed
back to him exclaiming: "That's another of Gomboust's scoundrelly tricks!"

Even now I don't know all the rights of that Saint-

Firmin Mineral Water Company, for I never had
the curiosity to read the documents concerning it,
which I found among my father's papers, and all of
which were stolen from me together with the rest of
the family records. But I have good reason to believe
that my mother did Gomboust no injustice when she
pronounced him miserly, rapacious, and unscrupu-
lous, in short, a bad lot; and it puzzles me now, when
I think of it, how it was that this unhappy man, who
was three parts blind and almost incapable of movement, cut off so to speak from the world, a burden
to himself and to others, this man who dwelt not
so much in a living body as in a coffin of flesh, should
be so enamoured of money as to commit acts of
treachery and cruelty for the sake of it.   What, in
heaven's name, was he going to do with his money?

There are some things that incline me to think
that from inexperience and sensitiveness my parents
exaggerated their responsibility in this matter of
The Saint-Firmin Mineral Water concern.   They
were the victims of legal and financial sharks.   Rampon, the obliging Rampon, deemed it his duty for-
sooth to come to the rescue of a distinguished medical practitioner and a worthy citizen and parent, and
he squeezed us dry.   In point of fact, it was no very
tremendous catastrophe, but it left us with nothing.
My mother's poor little bits of jewellery, not much
in the way of gold and less still in the way of dia-
monds and pearls, the odds and ends of the old

family plate, battered and dented, the sugar-basin
with the swan handles, the coffee-pot with my grandfather Saturnin Parmentier's crest upon it, the mas-
sive soup-ladle, all had to be pawned to pay the
lawyers' fees.

One day my father came home and said:

"Well, it's done; Le Mimeur is sold!"

Le Mimeur was a little farm near Chartres, and
it was the last bit of family property that my mother
had to call her own. I had been taken to Le Mimeur when I was quite a little boy, and all I remembered of it was a white butterfly on a bramble
hedge, the shrill flight of the dragon flies among the
wind-swayed reeds, a startled field mouse scamper-
ing along a wall, and a little greyish flower shaped
like a snout which my mother pointed out to me,
saying: "Look, Pierrot, isn't it pretty?" *

That summed up Le Mimeur for me, and it
seemed a strange, a cruel thing that the hedge, the
rushes, the blue grey flowers, the field mouse, the
butterfly and the dragon-flies should all be sold. I
could not quite see how the sale could be carried out.
But my father said it had been done, so there it was.
And I brooded within me on this sorrowful mystery.

Like all the other things, Le Mimeur went to Rampon, who, nevertheless, could not take it within him
into the next world. All dead men are paupers,
Gomboust, and Rampon, no less than the rest. If
I knew in what cemetery Gomboust lies buried, I

* It was probably the toad-flax.

would go and whisper these words among the grasses that cover his grave: "Where is now thy treasure?"

Thus it came about that, in my very earliest childhood, I learned to know what manner of men are lawyers, and usurers. They are an immortal race. All things about them suffer change. They alone hold true to type. Even as Rabelais portrayed them so they remain to-day. They are the same to their beak and claws, and even to their unintelligible jargon.

It was some five years after the dark days which I have described. Calmer times had supervened, and I was at school, and our master, M. Triaire, had been telling us about the Harpies in the Æneid. Those sinister fowl, those human headed vultures which, swooping down upon the table of the pious Æneas and his companions, snatched away the meat, defiled the victuals, and spread abroad a loathsome stench, I knew them right enough! More expert in such matters than my fellow scholars, I knew them for lawyers and hucksterers.

But how wholesome and pleasant is that cave of harpies, which Virgil describes for us as all befouled with dung and dripping flesh, compared with the office and green cardboard files of a man of law.

It is because I loathed and detested those murderous paper holders that I never could endure to have any files or filing cases about me. And so I have always mislaid my papers, my poor harmless papers.

CHAPTER XXI

THE PAPAGAY

HEN she came in with the coffee, old Mélanie informed us that the Comtesse Michaud's parrot had escaped. The people thought they could see it on M. Bellaguet's roof. I got up from the table and rushed to the window. In the courtyard a group, consisting of the concierge and a few domestics, were gazing upwards and pointing towards the gutter round the roof. My godfather, coffee-cup in hand, followed me to the window and asked where the popinjay was.

"There," said I, pointing upwards like the people in the yard.

But my godfather could not see it, and I could not show it him because I could not see it myself, and merely affirmed its presence there on the authority of others.

"And you, Madame Nozière, can you see the papagay?" asked my godfather.

"The papagay?"

"The papagay or the papegaut?"

"The papagay?"

"The papagay," repeated by godfather laughing.

163

His laughter sounded like little rippling bells and made his braces tinkle on his green silk waistcoat. His gaiety was infectious, and I kept on laughing and repeating, without knowing what I was saying:

"The papagay, the papagay!"

But my dear mamma, being of a prudent disposition, forbore to smile until my father informed her that the old name for the parrot was papagay or popingay.

"Gay as a papagay, as Rabelais says," said my godfather, by way of illustration.

At the name of Rabelais, which I then heard for the first time, I burst into fits of laughter, I don't know why—stupidity, silliness, tomfoolery, I suppose, for it certainly was not from any presentiment, intuition, or revelation of the sublime buffoonery, the merry whimsicality, the folly wiser than wisdom, that lies concealed beneath that name. Nevertheless, it cannot be gainsaid that it was a becoming manner in which to salute the creator of *Gargantua*. My dear mamma signed to me to hold my noise, and asked if there were any real grounds for saying that parrots were gay.

"Madame Nozière," my godfather made reply, "Papagay rhymes with gay. That is itself reason enough for the common run of men, who attach more importance to the sound of a word than they do to its meaning. Moreover, one may reasonably suppose that a parrot is pleased to see himself ar-

rayed in such a smart green dress. Is not the green
of a parrot's feathers usually called *'gay' green?"*

In the neighbourhood of my fifth year I had had
some little differences with Madame Laroque's parrot, Navarino; that I had not yet forgotten. He had
bitten my finger, and I had thought seriously about
giving him a dose of poison. We had made up our
quarrel, but I wasn't drawn to parrots. I had
learnt about their ways from a little book called
"Ernestine's Aviary," which I had had for a New
Year's gift, and which dealt with all the birds in the
space of a few pages. Anxiety to shine in conversation led me to say, on the authority of my book, that
the savage tribes of America feed on parrots.

"Its flesh must be dark and tough," objected my
godfather. "I have never heard that it was fit to
eat."

"What, Danquin," said my father. 'Don't you
remember the story about the Princess de Joinville
when she first came to the Tuileries from her home
in the Wild West? She had a cold and refused
chicken broth, demanding parrot broth instead."

My father had been hostile to the July Government, and even now, after the revolution of '48,
still retained a feeling of animosity towards Louis
Philippe's family. It was, therefore, with a spice
of malice that he launched this shaft, glancing the
while at my mother, who was rather inclined to pity
the lot of exiled princesses.

"Poor princesses," sighed she, "they pay dearly for the public honours accorded them.

All of a sudden I caught sight of the parrot in the gutter. I uttered a yell of triumph so savage that my mother was at first horrified, and then angry.

"There it is, mamma, look! there! there!"

"Do you know 'Greenie-Green,' Madame Noziére?" asked my godfather.

My mother shook her head.

"What, you don't know 'Greenie-Green?' Well, you've missed something."

"There's no time for reading, Monsieur Danquin, when you've got a child belonging to you that wears out his knickerbockers as if by magic. It's a piece of poetry, I suppose?"

"It is, Madame Nozière, and a very charming piece too."

> "At Nevers, then, in a convent cell
> A famous parrot once did dwell.
> His plumage was bright and fair to see,
> And his manners were gentle and frank and free
> As the ways of the young are wont to be."

The nuns loved him to distraction:

> "They petted him more, so I have heard,
> Than if he had been the king's own bird."

And then at night:

> He'd roost so snug on the Agnus box.

Greenie-Green used to talk like an angel. But—" and there my godfather stopped short.

"But what?" I asked.

My father at this juncture very properly remarked that I did not speak like an angel.

"But," my godfather went on, "he went away cruising on the Loire with bargees and musketeers, and his language suffered in consequence."

"You see," said my mother, pointing the moral, "how evil communications corrupt good manners."

"God-papa, is he dead—Greenie-Green?" I asked.

My godfather put on a most dismal countenance, and said in a psalm-droning voice:

"He died from eating too many sweets. Let him be a warning to greedy little children."

And my godfather gazing out on the court, which was all gold in the sunlight, smiled a melancholy smile.

"What radiant weather," said he. "The last bright days seem always the sorest to part with."

"They seem like a boon from heaven," said my mother. "The cold and dark days will soon be here now. This afternoon old Debas is coming to sweep the dining-room chimney." And thereupon she went off to her bedroom.

I can vividly remember the most trifling circumstances connected with the memorable events of that day.

My mother reappeared with her velvet bonnet tied under her chin, her mantle of puce-coloured silk, and her umbrella with the folding handle.

From her preoccupied and pensive air, I guessed
that she was going out to do some winter shopping
and that she was wondering how to lay out her
money to the best advantage, for she thought a lot
of her money, not for its own sake, but because her
husband had to work so hard to get it.   She bent
down her dear face which her bonnet enshrined as
though in a velvet jewel-case, kissed me on the forehead, told me to get on with my lessons, reminded
Mélanie to open a bottle of wine for M. Debas, and
went out.   My father and my godfather left the
house almost immediately after.

And so I was all by myself.   But, as usual, I did
not learn my lesson, being led away by instinct and
the inspiration of the potent spirit which governed
the workings of my mind.   It prompted me not to
learn my lessons, and indeed deprived me of all
opportunity of so doing by continually imposing upon
me other arduous tasks amazing in their diversity.

That afternoon it suggested in a manner not to
be denied that I should look out of the window and
watch for the truant parrot.   But it was in vain
that I kept staring up at the roofs and the chimney-
tops.   The parrot was nowhere to be seen.   I was
beginning to yawn with weariness when I suddenly
heard rather a loud noise behind me, and turning
round beheld M. Debas.   He had a bucket on his
head, and was carrying a ladder, a jug, a grappling
hook, some rope, and heaven knows what besides.

It must not be inferred therefrom that M. Debas
was a mason or a plumber. In point of fact, he was
a secondhand bookseller, who displayed his wares
in boxes on the parapet of the Quai Voltaire. My
mother had nicknamed him Simon de Nantua after
a pedlar about whom she used to make me read in
a little book that no one hears about nowadays.
Simon de Nantua used to go up and down the country visiting all the fairs. He bore a canvas pack on
his back and indulged in endless moralizings. He
was always in the right. His story bored me cruelly,
and left a most dismal impression on my memory,
but, nevertheless, it was instrumental in enabling me
to recognize one important truth, and that is that
it does not do to be always in the right. M. Debas,
like Simon de Nantua, moralized from morning till
night, and occupied himself with everything save
his own business. Always ready to oblige his neighbours, and to do odd jobs for all and sundry, he
would put up or take down stoves, rivet broken
crockery, fit new handles to knives, see to the bells,
grease the locks, regulate timepieces, help people to
move out or to move in, give first aid to folk rescued
from drowning, fix draught excluders to windows
and doors, hold forth at the wine merchant's in favour of constituted authority, and sing of a Sunday
in the chapel of the Little Sisters of the Poor. My
mother looked upon him as a good man who was
superior to his station in life. As for me, I should

have found it difficult to put up with the everlasting sermons on seemliness and good behaviour with which M. Debas was continually plaguing me, had it not been that he amused me enormously with an excessive ardour for work, a trait of which I was the only person in the world to see the comic side. Whenever I saw him, I always counted on being entertained by some amazing piece of excitement. Nor on this occasion were my expectations falsified.

Our dining-room stove was of white earthenware, cracked and split in various places. It stood in a recess in a corner of the room. It was fitted with a pipe, likewise of earthenware, surmounted by the head of a bearded man, which, because I had heard the information given to M. Debas, I knew to be that of Jupiter Trophonius. And the beard of so august a deity duly impressed me. M. Debas put on a white overall and mounted the steps. And lo! in a trice, Jupiter Trophonius was lying on the floor, and from the column from which he had been dismounted the soot was pouring in volumes. The stove itself, now taken to pieces, was strewn in little bits all over the floor, and clouds of ashes darkened the air. The gloom was still further intensified by an impalpable powder which ascended to the ceiling, and slowly descended again to settle in a thick layer on the furniture and the carpet. M. Debas was mixing mortar which was running all over the side of his bucket. It was quite evident that he enjoyed labouring after the manner of the god who wrought order out of chaos. At this juncture Mélanie came in, her basket on her arm. She gazed from wall to wall, and from ceiling to floor in dismay, and with a deep sigh exclaimed:

"How in the world am I going to lay dinner in here?"

Then, apparently despairing of a satisfactory reply, she went out to get on with her shopping.

Chaos was still reigning when suddenly there was a fresh outbreak of excitement in the courtyard. M. Bellaguet's coachman, old Alexandre, our concierge, the Caumont's servant and young Alphonse, all began to shout at once:

"There it is. I see it. There it is!"

This time I caught sight of it right enough. There, on the top of the roof, was the Comtesse Michaud's parrot. It was green, with a splash of red on the wings. But scarcely had it shown itself when it disappeared again.

The people in the court were arguing about the direction it had taken. One thought it had flown towards M. Bellaguet's garden, the idea being that it would be reminded of the Brazilian forests in which it had spent its early days. Another swore it had made for the quay, so that it could cast itself into the river. The concierge had seen it perch on the tower of Saint-Germain-des-Prés. But the old concierge had served under Napoleon, and his recollection of the eagle with the national colours had evidently acted upon his imagination. The Comtesse Michaud's parrot was not flying, from one church tower to another. M. Caumont's clerk conjectured with greater probability that, driven by stress of hunger, the fugitive was making for the roof that concealed its food supply. Simon de Nantua, leaning against the window, was lending a thoughtful ear to what was passing. In order to display my knowledge, I remarked to him that this parrot was not such a fine one as Greenie-Green.

"Greenie-Green, what do you call Greenie-Green?" said he.

My bosom swelled with pride as I informed him that Greenie-Green was a parrot belonging to the Visitandines of Nevers, which used to speak like an angel, but which had got to use bad language after travelling up and down the Loire in the company of bargees and musketeers. As soon as I had said it, I realized that it is a mistake to air one's knowledge to the ignorant, for Simon de Nantua, having glared at me severely with a pair of big eyes about as expressive as lamp globes, rebuked me for talking rubbish.

Meanwhile, he was revolving deep thoughts within his breast.

Among the countless services that his kindness of heart prompted him to render his neighbours, the one which he loved best to perform was that of re-

capturing escaped birds. For example, he had often
brought back Madame Caumont's canaries. He
deemed that to restore her parrot to the Comtesse
Michaud was his bounden duty, and he did not hesi-
tate to take steps to accomplish it. Having hastily
replaced his white overall by an old green frock-coat
which was turning yellow like the autumn leaves, he
acquainted me with his intention, and, leaving the
dining-room in the chaotic condition which he had
not had time to reduce to order, he went out, his
head full of his scheme. I tore after him down
the staircase. At a bound we covered the short
space that separated us from the house I knew so
well, the house where Morin was concierge, the
house where the Comtesse Michaud lived. We flew
upstairs as far as the second floor landing, found
the door wide open, and entered to behold an air
of desolation over all. In the dining-room we saw
the deserted perch. Mathilde, the Countess's lady's
maid, explained the circumstances which had pre-
ceded and led up to Jacquot's flight. The day before, about five o'clock in the afternoon, a grey cat,
with short fur, an enormous great tom, whose depre-
dations had long since earned him an unfavourable
reputation, had come bounding into the dining-room.
At the sight of him Jacquot, in terror, had flown
out on to the landing, and escaped through the skylight. Twice did Mathilde relate this story. As
she was about to repeat it a third time, I slipped

out into the drawing-room and fell to gazing at the
full length portrait of General Comte Michaud
which occupied the principal panel. As I have
already mentioned, the General was depicted in full
dress, white breeches and patent leather boots, at
the battle of Wagram. At his feet were fragments
of shell, a cannon ball, a smoking grenade. In the
background soldiers, quite small by reason of their
being so far off, were charging. On his broad chest
the General wore the ribbon of the Grand Eagle
of the Legion of Honour, and the Cross of St.
Louis. I saw no incongruity in his wearing the
Cross of St. Louis at Wagram. I should have
done, when I saw the picture at a dealer's some years
later, if I had not been told that General Comte
Michaud, having been overwhelmed with favours
and distinctions by the Bourbons had, in 1816, caused
the cross to be added to his portrait. Simon de
Nantua aroused me from my reverie, and informed
me that people did not go into drawing-rooms without being asked and without first wiping their feet.
His reprimand was brief, for time was precious.

"Come on!" he said.

And armed with a thick rope, from which apparently he intended to suspend himself in mid air,
he mounted the staircase. I followed carrying a
glass which he had given into my charge, and which
contained some bread soaked in wine as a bait for
Jacquot. My heart beat violently at the thought

of the dangers into which this expedition was about
to plunge me. Never in their most thrilling adventures of warfare or the chase did the trappers of
Arkansas, the filibusters of South America, or the
buccaneers of St. Domingo, feel more keenly than I
the intoxication of peril. We mounted the staircase as far as it went, then we began on one of the
steepest of steep ladders, up which we struggled as
far as a skylight, through which Simon de Nantua
thrust one half of his body. I could now only see
his legs and his enormous posterior. First he called
Jacquot in wheedling tones, then he imitated Jacquot's raucous notes in case, I take it, the bird preferred the sound of his own organ to the speech of
man. Now he whistled, now he sang like a siren,
interrupting his incantations from time to time to
impart to me precepts in matters ranging from etiquette to ethics, and to instruct me how to blow my
nose in company, and how to comport myself towards the powers that be.

The hours went by. As the sun declined, the
shadows of the chimneys along the roofs grew longer
and longer. We were just beginning to despair,
when Jacquot hove in sight. The forecast of M.
Caumont's clerk was in a fair way to being brought
to pass. I thrust my head through the skylight, and
saw the parrot. He was coming along with difficulty, balancing his bulky body, and slowly and gin-
gerly descending the sloping roof of the gable. It

was he right enough, and he was making his way towards me. I could not keep still for joy. He was now quite close up. I did not dare to breathe. Simon de Nantua hailed him in rousing tones, and, taking the piece of bread soaked in wine, put it on to his closed fist and held it out to him at arm's length. Jacquot stopped short, darted a mistrustful glance in our direction, turned back, flapped his wings, and flew away. At first his flight was laboured, but gradually it grew more rapid and sustained, and, at length, carried him as far as the roof of a neighbouring house, where he disappeared from view. The discomfiture of both of us was great, but Simon de Nantua was not going to let himself be beaten by a bit of bad luck. He stretched forth his arm towards the ocean of roofs.

"After him!" he cried.

This masterful gesture, this short, sharp utterance carried me away. I hung on to his old frock-coat and, to relate the facts as they present themselves to my recollection, I clove the air with him and descended from the cloudy heights into an unknown enclosure wherein there rose up façades of carved stone. And I beheld a multitude of naked men; huge, terrifying figures, floating in a sunless sky. Some were upstaying there the weight of their mighty frames, others were falling in desperate headlong flight towards the dark verge where hideous demons were waiting to seize them. This

vision filled me with a sort of religious terror. My
sight grew dim, my legs gave way beneath me. Such
are the facts as they appeared to my senses
and my understanding and as they remain graven
on my memory, and faithful is the account of them
I have here set down. Howbeit, if these facts are
to be subjected to the laws of the higher criticism
I must add that we, Simon de Nantua and I, had
apparently descended the staircase with lightning
rapidity, run along the quay, turned down the Rue
Bonaparte and come to the École des Beaux-Arts
where, through a half-open door, I caught sight of
a copy of Michael Angelo's "Last Judgment"
painted by Sigalon. This is only a hypothesis, but
it is a likely one. And now, without further com-
mitting ourselves to anything definite on this point,
let us continue our narrative. I had only a moment
to contemplate the floating giants, when I found myself, with Simon de Nantua at my side, in a spacious
quadrangle around which were to be seen beadles in
cocked hats, and young men with long hair shadowed
by wide-brimmed felts à la Rubens, and carrying
portfolios under their arms. The beadles said they
had seen nothing of the Comtesse Michaud's parrot.
The young men jocularly told Simon de Nantua to
put some salt on its tail if he wanted to catch it, or,
better still, to scratch its head. They swore that
there was nothing parrots liked better. And with a

bow the young men begged us to present their compliments to the Comtesse Michaud.

"Saucy young cubs!" said Simon de Nantua, and he quitted the place in a huff.

Returning to the Comtesse Michaud's, we went into the dining-room, and found—what do you suppose? The parrot himself back on his perch. He was riding it with an unruffled, easy-going air, and looked as though he had never left it. A few grains of hempseed that lay scattered about the floor bore witness to the fact that he had just had a meal. At our approach, he turned on us an eye that was as round and defiant as a cockade, swung to and fro on his perch, ruffled his feathers, and opened wide the beak whose curve determined the outline of his whole countenance. An old lady, wearing a black lace cap, her thin cheeks framed in white curls, doubtless the Comtesse Michaud, was seated near Jacquot. At the sight of us she looked the other way. The lady's maid went in and out of the room without vouchsafing a word. Simon de Nantua kept fiddling about with his hat, holding it first in one hand, then in the other. He pretended to smile, but only looked silly. At last Mathilde informed us, without deigning to cast a look in our direction, that Jacquot had just returned of his own accord, having come in through the skylight in the attic where she slept, and which the dear creature knew so well from having so often been carried thither on his Mathilde's shoulder.

"He would have come back all the sooner," she added sourly, "if you hadn't frightened him away."

They did not ask us to stay, and, as Simon de Nantua ruefully remarked to me as we were going down the stairs, they did not so much as offer us a little refreshment.

It was getting dark when I returned home. I found the whole household in a state of consternation; my mother was feverishly excited, old Mélanie in tears, my father doing his best to appear calm. They thought I had been kidnapped by gipsies or travelling circus folk, or taken up by the police outside some shop with a crowd of hooligans, or at the very least that I was lost and wandering about in some far-off maze of streets. They had been to find out whether I was at Madame Caumont's, or at the Laroques' or at Madame Letord's, the printseller's. They had even gone to M. Clérot's, the mapseller's, where I sometimes liked to wander to contemplate a globe representing this earth, whereon I deemed that I occupied no unimportant place. They were just thinking, when I rang the bell, of going off to notify the police. My mother looked at me very carefully all over, touched my forehead and found it moist, ran her fingers through my tangled hair that was full of cobwebs, and said,

"But where have you been, to come home in such

a state, without your hat, and a great hole in the knee of your knickerbockers?"

I recounted my adventure, and how I had gone with Simon de Nantua to look for the parrot.

"Well," she cried. "I should never have thought M. Debas would dare to keep the child out the whole afternoon without my permission and without letting anyone know."

"You must put it down to his ignorance!" said old Mélanie, with a toss of her head. Mélanie was a good soul, but being humble and lowly she was inclined to be down on her own class.

Dinner was served in the drawing-room, the dining-room being totally out of the question.

"Pierre," said my father, when I had finished my soup, "how was it you did not realize how terribly anxious your mother would be at your being out all that long time?"

I had to undergo a little more scolding, but, obviously, it was Simon de Nantua who was regarded as the chief culprit.

My mother kept asking me about my climbing adventures, and seemed unable to shake off her terror at the dangers I had been through.

I answered her that I had not been in any danger. I tried to calm her, but, at the same time, I was anxious to give proof of my powers and courage, and, while I kept repeating that I had been careful to run no risk, I represented myself as mounting ladders suspended in space, scaling walls, clambering over precipitous roofs, and careering along gutters. At first, as she listened to my tale, a slight tremulousness of the lips betrayed her emotion. Then, gradually recovering her serenity, she tossed her head and finally burst out laughing in my face. I had overdone it. And, when I told her how I had seen a host of enormous naked men suspended in mid-air, they put on the closure and sent me to bed.

The adventure of the parrot became famous in our family and among our friends. My dear mamma used to tell, not perhaps without a touch of motherly pride, how I had raced along the house tops in company with M. Debas, whom she never forgave. My godfather used to dub me ironically "the parrot hunter;" M. Dubois himself, notwithstanding his habitually grave demeanour, almost smiled as he listened to so strange a story, and remarked that with his green coat, his big head, his short thick neck, his wide chest, squat figure and grim aspect, the warlike parrot on his perch offers a pretty close likeness to Napoleon on board the *Northumberland*. And M. Marc Ribert too, when he heard this story, M. Marc Ribert, the long-haired romanticist whose clothes were of velvet, and who was given to dallying with the Muses, would begin to murmur:

"In the springtime, pretty ring time,
There is naught so gay, I ween,
As the plumage of the parrot
Blue, grey, yellow, red and green."

CHAPTER XXII

UNCLE HYACINTHE

NE day when I went into the drawingroom, I was very much taken aback to find my mother in conversation with a rather fine-looking old man, whom I had never seen before. His bare pate, encircled with a coronal of silver hairs, was pink in hue. His complexion was clear, his eyes blue, and a smile hovered about his lips. He looked spruce and well shaven, and a pair of mutton-chop whiskers befringed his chubby cheeks. He was wearing a bunch of violets in the buttonhole of his great coat.

"Is this your little chap, Antoinette?" he asked when he saw me. "You'd take him for a girl, he looks so soft and shy. You must give him plenty of plum pudding if you're going to make a man of him."

He signed to me to draw near, and laid his hand on my shoulder

"Little man," he began, "you're just at the age when life seems all smiles and caresses. One day you'll find out that life is often hard and occasionally unjust and cruel. For your sake I hope you won't have to learn the lesson in too harsh a school. But let me tell you this, and never forget it, that a stout heart and a clear conscience will bring you through anything."

Honesty and kindness seemed to beam in his face. His voice went straight to your heart. It was impossible not to be moved as he looked at you with eyes that melted as he spoke.

"*Mon enfant*," he went on, "Fortune has blessed you with excellent parents who, when the time comes, will give you their guidance in the difficult task of choosing a career. Wouldn't you like to be a soldier?"

My mother answered for me, and said she didn't think so.

"It's a fine calling, though," the old fellow rattled on. "One day, without food and without shelter, the soldier flings himself down like a beggar on a bed of straw, the next night he sups in a palace, and the highest ladies in the land deem it an honour to wait on him. He is familiar with every change of fortune, with every mode of life. But if ever you should have the honour to wear a soldier's uniform, remember, my son, that it is a soldier's duty to protect the widow and the orphan, and to spare the vanquished foe. He who speaks these words to you bore arms under Napoleon the Great. Alas, more than thirty years have now rolled by since the god of battles quitted this earth, and now that he is gone there is no one left to rally our eagles to the conquest of the world. Ah, my son, don't be a soldier."

He pushed me gently from him, and, turning to my mother, resumed the conversation which my appearance had interrupted.

"Oh, yes, yes, just a modest little place; something after the style of a gamekeeper's cottage. Well, then, it's settled, and, thanks to you, my dear Antoinette I shall be able to have what I have always longed for. After all the disappointments and the ups and downs of life I shall taste the delights of repose. I require so little to live on. I have always hoped that I should be able to end my days in the peace of the country."

He rose, kissed my mother's hand with a gallant air, nodded affectionately at me, and took his departure. His mien was noble and his step was firm.

I was much surprised when I learned that this amiable old gentleman was Uncle Hyacinthe, whom I had never heard mentioned save in terms of horror and reprobation, who brought with him disaster and despair wherever he went, when, in short, I heard that he was indeed that same Uncle Hyacinthe who was the terror and black sheep of the family. My parents had refused him the house; but Hyacinthe, after ten years' silence, had, in a touching letter, just announced to my mother that he intended retiring to some hamlet in his native county if she would provide money to pay his fare and set him up in a little home of his own. Once there, he said, he could support himself by managing the estates of a foster brother with whom he had always remained on excellent terms. My mother, all too ready to believe his tale, and deaf to my father's advice, agreed to lend him the money.

Some little time afterwards she learnt that, having squandered in riotous living the funds received by him for a different purpose, he had got a job as bookkeeper and accountant at the establishment of a *marchand d'hommes* in the Rue Saint-Honoré. Such was the name given to those who, for valuable consideration provided rich young men anxious to evade military service, with men to take their place. These gentry did a roaring trade, but they were held in scant esteem, and members of their staff could hardly aspire to be greatly looked up to. They congregated for the most part in a big house in the Rue Saint-Honoré at the corner of the Rue du Coq, which was covered from top to bottom with signs adorned with *croix d'honneur* and tricolour flags. On the ground floor was a shop where they sold second-hand epaulettes and N.C.O. stripes, and a bar frequented by soldiers who had completed the seven years' service required of them by the State, and desired to rejoin the colours. Outside, by way of signboard, there hung a picture painted on a piece of sheet iron, representing two grenadiers

seated at a table in an arbour, each of them pulling
the stopper from his jar of beer with so free and
lucky a sweep of the arm that each jet of the foam-
ing liquor, after describing a bold curve in the air,
descended neatly into his comrade's glass. It was
there, I am afraid, behind a pair of frowsy curtains,
that Uncle Hyacinthe busied himself with his new
duties, which consisted in making the discharged
soldiers gamble and drink so as to render them care-
less as to the price of their re-engagement. Perhaps,
when I passed by this house in the Rue Saint-Honoré,
it was the gaiety of the sign that helped me to bear
with equanimity the sight of the dram shop in which
the good name of the family was being dragged in
the mire.

Hyacinthe who, albeit no scholar, was good at
figures and a quick reckoner had, what used to be
called in those days, a good hand. That is to say
he was a skilful penman. One conspicuous example
of his work was a copy of Bonaparte's proclamation
to the troops in Italy. It was written in microscopic
characters, and the lines were so arranged as to
form a portrait of the First Consul. He became a
conscript in 1813, and was promoted to the rank of
adjutant the following year, during the campaign in
France. He used to boast of having had a conversation with the Emperor one night, when the army
was bivouacking near Craonne.

"Sire," said Hyacinthe, "we will shed our last drop

of blood under your leadership, for you are the living symbol of Freedom and of our native land."

"Hyacinthe," replied the Emperor, "you have read me aright."

Our only knowledge of this interview, let me hasten to add, is derived from the account given of it by Hyacinthe himself, who, we have his own word for it, covered himself with glory next day at Craonne. As the most splendid deeds occasionally bring about the most undesirable results, it came to pass that Hyacinthe, having blossomed out into a hero in the space of a few moments, considered he had earned a lifelong emancipation from all those rules and obligations by which ordinary folk are encumbered, and thenceforward respected neither God nor man. He had squandered all his virtue in a single day. It is doubtful whether he was at Waterloo, and this point will probably never be settled. Even at this early stage he was a great haunter of taverns and would rather talk about his exploits than repeat them. When, in 1815, he was just completing his twenty-second year, he got his discharge. A handsome, strapping, upstanding blade, he was the darling of the sex and no feminine heart was proof against his blandishments. He was beloved by one of my mother's aunts, a well-to-do yeoman's daughter. He consented to marry her and played ducks and drakes with her money. By betraying, ill-treating and deserting her he afforded her numerous opportunities of proving how fervently she idolized, how madly she loved him. Careful, even stingy, with her money, she would simply throw it away where he was concerned. He might have been seen at this period, between Paris and Pontoise, wearing a grey hat with a steel buckle and a very broad crown, a green frock-coat with gold buttons, nankeen breeches and patent leather top boots, driving a two-wheeled dog-cart, altogether an admirable subject for a picture by Carle Vernet. Frequenting the *Bœuf à la Mode* and the *Rocher de Cancale,* in the company of women of the town, and passing his nights in brothels and gambling dens, it only took him a few years to get through his wife's property—fields, meadows, woods, mill and all. Having reduced the poor devoted thing to beggary, he abandoned her, to go off on a career of adventure with a man named Huguet who had once been a postmaster. Huguet was an ill-dressed, bandy-legged, dried-up little wisp of a man whom Hyacinthe made his servant, his partner and sometimes, when there were any risks to be run, his employer. Huguet was a rogue and had swindled people right and left, but to Hyacinthe he showed himself the most faithful, the most generous and the noblest of friends. Huguet, who was a Royalist and a bit of a firebrand, and who, moreover, had brought the White Terror into Aveyron, his native place, turned Bonapartist because of his regard for his beloved Hyacinthe, who was a Bonapartist because it

paid him. Hyacinthe dressed for the part. He wore
a long frock-coat buttoned up to the chin, a bunch
of violets in his buttonhole and carried a club
in his hand. On the Boulevard de Gand, surrounded by a few brothers in arms, and Huguet
following behind like a spaniel, he used to anathema-
tize England for keeping Napoleon in captivity and
when he came out of the tavern he would face north-
west and pointing an avenging finger toward *la
perfide Albion* denounce her monstrous conduct.
His lips moved in silent prayer for the advent of the
Kingdom of the Son of Man. If he met some loyal
subject of the King decorated with a silver lily he
would give an inaudible grunt and say, "There goes
another companion of Ulysses." If he could lay hold
of a dog without being seen, he would tie a white
cockade on to its tail. But he never got involved in
plots or conspiracies. He did not even fight duels.
Uncle Hyacinthe was like Panurge. He had a natural dislike to being hit. Huguet supplied the pluck
and was always ready for a set-to. Being reduced to
living by his wits, Hyacinthe set up as a professor
of writing and bookkeeping in the Rue Montmatre.
Huguet scrubbed the floor and grilled the sausages,
and Hyacinthe, while waiting for the pupils to come,
operated on the quills like a master in the art, placing
the point on his left thumbnail so that he might
bring down the knife with the skill of an adept and
make the requisite slit. But in vain he sat and

trimmed his quills, in vain a notice, writ in round-hand copper plate, Gothic and sloping, hung up at the front door enumerated the various diplomas of the expert caligraphist and certificated accountant. Not a pupil came. Then he started as an agent for a life insurance company. His fine presence and persuasive address would have brought him many clients, but wine and women accounted for his initial profits and prevented him from getting any subsequent ones, and this, despite the zeal displayed by Huguet, who did the touting on his friend's behalf, but met with no success because he squinted horribly, reeked of wine, and had a stammering tongue, and because persuasion abode not within his lips. After this set back the two cronies set up a fencing school in a plaster-caste maker's studio at Montrouge. Hyacinthe was the master, Huguet his assistant. As the moulder continued to make use of the studio in his own hours, the plaster which filled the chinks in the floor rose up at every assault, covered the feet of the fencers and enveloped them in a cloud of pungent dust which made them weep and sneeze beneath their masks. It was wine and women again that put an end to this attempt to follow the noble profession of arms. After trying a few other lines of business of which no record remains, Hyacinthe conceived the brilliant idea of exploiting "The Elixir of the Old Man of the Mountain," prepared in accordance with the formula of Dr. Gibet. Huguet distilled the liquor and Hyacinthe "placed" it with the grocers and chemists. But this partnership was brief and looked as if it was going to have an ugly sequel, for the police began to suspect that "Gibet, Doctor of Medicine," was nothing but a fraud. It is believed in some quarters that Huguet, the distiller, had a month or two's experience of prison life over the business. Hyacinthe then placed his faculties at the service of the State and became a market inspector. He exercised his functions at night, but he was more often found in the tavern than at his post, and, although his friend Huguet did his best to understudy him, he was several times reprimanded and finally dismissed. This decision was regarded as a political measure. In the person of Hyacinthe the authorities were persecuting one of Napoleon's old soldiers. This gained him the assistance of certain liberals who procured him a berth as a copyist and he thought no small beer of himself when he had to copy "Les Plaideurs sans procès," a three-act comedy in verse by M. Étienne. "M. Étienne," said Hyacinthe, "deserves less kudos for having got into the Institute by merit than for being turned out of it again by a King." It is, of course, a fact that in 1816 Étienne was expelled from the Institute after its reorganization. Meanwhile, at Hyacinthe's instigation, Huguet took up the wine trade and defrauded the Customs, which earned him some five thousand francs profit and six months in gaol. "Not the worst

bit of business I have done by a long chalk," said
Huguet, on reflection. Such cynicism was revolting
to the hero of Craonne, who had principles, professed the moral code of the Savoyard vicar supple-
mented by the sense of military honour and incul-
cated in Huguet, over their potations, what he owed
to duty and the law. "Keep to the narrow path, or
get back to it if you have strayed from it. Innocence
or repentance," such was the old soldier's motto.
Huguet, as he listened to him, gazed at him in admiration and wept into his glass. Seeing him thus
rehabilitated by repentance, Hyacinthe joined him
in the formation of a company for the distribution
of books and printed matter in the city of Paris.
It did not prove a success. It was, I think,
shortly after this discomfiture that Hyacinthe came
to interview my mother, as I have already related,
and became secretary to a *marchand d'hommes*.

His enterprises had one thing in their favour:
they were very short lived. He did not remain long
buying men at the sign of The Two Grenadiers.
No one knows what he did after that. His final oc-
cupation was the only one known to his family.
Hyacinthe, who by this time was a very old man,
opened an office in the back room of a tavern in the
Rue Rambuteau. Seated at a table with a bottle of
white wine and a bag of roasted chestnuts in front
of him, he gave advice to the little local tradesfolk
as to how to get out of paying their debts and avoid

legal proceedings. I don't know whether I have mentioned it, but Uncle Hyacinthe was a genius at chicanery. This trait gives the finishing touch to his portrait. Cunning, tricky, familiar with all the tortuosities of legal procedure, he could have given points to Chicaneau himself. The sight of a writ caused him to rub his hands with glee. In his little back office he also acted as secretary to the female domestics round about. His friend Huguet, shrivelled up, lame but still alert, had not forsaken him. They slept in an outhouse behind the tavern. Huguet taxed all his resources to keep his friend's pipe charged with tobacco. One night he was stabbed between the shoulders in an affray with some roughs. He was taken to the hospital, where Hyacinthe went to visit him. Huguet smiled on him and gave up the ghost. Hyacinthe returned to his labours, drawing up leases and acting as counsel and secretary to distressful shopkeepers and lovelorn scullery-maids. But his beautiful handwriting began to get shaky, his sight drew dim and his head nodded. For hours at a stretch he would sit dozing and vacant. Six weeks after Huguet's death, he fell down in an apoplectic fit. They took him away to the house in the Rue du Sabot where his poor wife was living in a single room. She had not set eyes on him for forty years, but she loved him just as dearly as on their wedding day. She nursed him with the most loving care. Paralysed all down his left side and dragging one leg, he scarcely ever moved and hardly said a word. Every morning she would help him from his bed to the window where he would sit the whole day looking towards the sun. She filled his pipe for him and her eyes never left him. Six months later he had a second stroke and lived for six days unable to move. His speech had quite gone, he could only mutter unintelligible sounds; but just as he was dying they thought they could hear him calling out for Huguet.

My father never mentioned Uncle Hyacinthe's name. My mother avoided speaking of him. Nevertheless, she often told the following story which, in her eyes, summed up the frivolous and deceitful character of the man.

It was at the time of the Revolution of 1830. Hyacinthe, though past his fortieth year, was still a man about town, and home life bored him. During the *Trois Glorieuses* he lay low hoping the people would win the day. On the 30th July, after the defection of the royal troops, when the firing had quite ceased, and the tricolour was floating over the Tuileries, our gentleman ventured to show his nose out of doors. For reasons best known to himself, he wanted to get to a place at the corner of the Bastille and the Faubourg Saint-Antoine. He was living at the time near the Barrière de l'Étoile, an out-of-the-way and lonely place. To achieve his object he would either have had to foot it, beneath a scorching sun,

along streets with the pavement torn up, and get past
more than thirty barricades guarded by the people,
or he would have had to go a long way round
through some very unsafe quarters of the city. To
get over the difficulty Hyacinthe bethought him of
an ingenious device. He betook himself to a neighbour of his who kept a little eating house, soaked a
piece of linen in some rabbit's blood, tied it round
his head and got the landlord and a boy to carry him
up to the first barricade, which was hard by on the
Faubourg du Roule. As he had anticipated, the men
guarding the barricade thought he had been wounded. They took him from his bearers and conveyed
him past the obstacle with every possible care. That
done, they gave him a glass of wine and picked out
two of their number to carry him along on a
stretcher. A procession formed and increased in
numbers as they went along. A student from the
École Polytechnique marched at its head with drawn
sword. Some working men with their shirt sleeves
rolled up and sprigs of evergreen thrust into their
rifle barrels, marched on either side of the stretcher
shouting:

"Honour the brave!"

Some printers' apprentices, recognizable by their
paper caps, bakers' men clad all in white, schoolboys wearing the epaulettes and leather trappings of
the Guard, an urchin of ten in a shako that came

right down over his ears, brought up the rear and kept calling out:

"Honour the brave!"

Women knelt down as they passed, others tossed flowers to the stricken hero and laid tricolour ribbons and laurel branches on the stretcher. At the corner of the Rue Saint-Florentin, a grocer of liberal convictions delivered himself of an harangue and presented him with a medal stamped with a figure of La Fayette. As the procession hove in sight, the defenders of the barricades dragged paving stones, casks, carts and everything out of the way in order to clear a passage for the wounded man. All along the route the rebel sentries presented arms, drums beat a salute, bugles sounded. Shouts of "Hurrah for the people's defender. Hurrah for the supporter of the Charter! Long live the champion of Liberty" mounted up through a glare of dust and sunlight to a brazen sky. At every drink-shop glasses filled with ruby liquid flew to the lips of the unknown hero stretched on his couch of glory, and whole bottles went to slake the thirst of his bearers who were smoking like cassolettes.

And Uncle Hyacinthe was deposited with honour in the shop of Madame Constance, laundress, at the corner of the Place de la Bastille and the Faubourg Saint-Antoine.

CHAPTER XXIII

BARA

HAT I find fault with," said my mother, after recounting this episode of a disreputable career "is that Hyacinthe, by this piece of trickery, usurped the prerogatives of misfortune and counterfeited a victim."

"He ran a big risk in so doing," said my godfather. "The popular enthusiasm he had excited would have immediately turned to fury if he had been found out. He would have been treated with ignominy by those who had honoured him as a noble citizen and he might have been torn to pieces by the furies who had given him drink. An armed mob is capable of any outrage. Nevertheless it must be allowed that the Parisian populace displayed much restraint during the *Trois Glorieuses* and in no wise abused their victory. The wealthy middle classes and the learned societies fought side by side with working men; the students of the École Polytechnique did a great deal to make success a certainty. And for the most part they distinguished themselves by acts of heroism and humanity.

"One of them, who made his way into the Château

at the head of a band of popular troops, called on the Royal Guards to surrender. They held the butt-end of their rifles in the air in token of submission, but the old captain who commanded them rushed furiously, sword in hand, upon the Polytechnique student. The latter, just as the sword was at his breast, turned it aside and managed to wrest it away. He then returned it to the officer saying, 'Monsieur, take back this sword which you have wielded with honour on so many fields of battle but which you will never more employ against the people.' The Captain, overcome with admiration and gratitude, removed the Cross of the Legion of Honour from his tunic and presented it to his young adversary saying, 'Doubtless the country will one day confer this decoration upon you. Permit me now to offer you the *insignia*.' In this civil struggle, it was the sentiment of honour and patriotism that diminished the bitterness between the combatants."

My godfather had scarcely finished his story when M. Marc Ribert began on another:

"On the 28th July," he said, "when the Parisian troops on the Place de l'Hôtel-de-Ville were becoming demoralized under a heavy fire, a young man, bearing a tricolour flag fixed to the point of a lance, rushed forward to within ten paces of the Garde Royale crying, 'Citizens, see how sweet it is to die for freedom!' And he fell, riddled with bullets."

My mother, touched at the recital of these heroic

deeds, asked how it was that such noble acts were not more generally known and more widely celebrated.

My godfather gave many reasons:

"The wars of the Monarchy, of the Revolution and of the Empire have saturated the history of France with acts of heroism, so that there is no room for any more. Besides, the glory attaching to the conquerors of July is obliterated by the insignificance of their success. They did but bring about the triumph of mediocrity, and the dynasty that came into being as a result of their devotion never cared to recall its origins, so, you see, even heroes are not immune from the caprices of destiny."

"Possibly," said my mother, "yet it is a great pity that a noble deed should sink into oblivion."

On hearing this, old M. Dubois, who had been toying with his snuff-box during the whole conversation, turned his great calm countenance upon my mother.

"Do not be too eager to tax Fate with injustice, Madame Noziére. All these brave deeds, all these fine speeches, are but fables and empty hearsay. If it is impossible to give an accurate account of things said and done in an attentive and orderly assembly, is one likely, my dear madame, to be able to take stock of a gesture or a speech amid the tumult of a combat. It matters little to me, gentlemen, that your stories are imaginary and without any foundation in fact; what is of prime importance is that their whole conception is alien alike to Nature and to Art, they lack the beautiful simplicity that is the sole preservative against the corrosion of time. That is why we should let them moulder undisturbed in those back Christmas numbers in which they lie embalmed. Historic truth is not concerned with those magnificent examples of heroism that are bandied about from mouth to mouth, from one generation to another; they have no existence outside the realms of Art and Poetry. I know not whether Bara, the youth whose life the Chouans promised to spare on condition that he shouted, 'Long live the King,' actually shouted 'Long live the Republic,' and so fell pierced by a score of bayonets as a reward— I know not, nor ever shall know. But I do know that the picture of the child, laying down his life, still in its very flower, for Freedom's sake, brings tears into our eyes and fire into our hearts, and that no more perfect symbol of sacrifice could possibly be imagined. I know, too, I know above all, that when David, the sculptor, brings this child before me in all his pure and charming artlessness, giving himself up to death with the serenity of the stricken amazon in the Vatican, his cockade clasped to his bosom, and in his death-cold hand one of the drumsticks with which he had been sounding the charge, the miracle is wrought, the boy-hero is created, Bara lives, Bara is immortal!"

CHAPTER XXIV

MÉLANIE

BOUT this time a cruel blow fell upon me. Mélanie began to fail. Up to then, the different ages of man had only affected me by their amusing diversity. Old age I liked because it was picturesque, sometimes comic and easy to make fun of; I had yet to learn that it was burdensome and sad. Yes, Mélanie was growing old! Her basket began to weigh over-heavily on her arm, and when she came in from her shopping, you could hear her troubled breathing from the foot of the stairs through all the rooms. Her eyes were dim, dimmer than the ever-clouded glasses of her spectacles, and they were growing weaker day by day. Her failing sight caused her to make mistakes which at first made me laugh, but which soon began to distress me, so frequent and so woeful they became. She would take the lump of beeswax she kept to polish the floor for a crust of bread, and a soiled duster for the chicken she had just plucked. One day, thinking to sit down on her stool, she sat down instead on a toy theatre my godfather had given me. She was so mortally terrified at the crash that she forgot all about saying

she was sorry. Her memory was going; she mixed up the different periods of her life. She would talk about the open-air ball that took place at the Emperor's Coronation when she danced with the Mayor of the village, and tell how, at the time of the invasion, she had refused, at some peril to herself, to kiss a Cossack who was billeted at the farm, referring to these events as if they had just recently happened. She repeated the same stories over and over again, and was everlastingly telling us how bitterly cold the weather was on the 15th December, 1840, when the Emperor was brought back to Paris from St. Helena. His *petit chapeau* and his sword had been placed on his coffin. She had seen them, but nevertheless, she did not believe that he was dead. She began to worry herself and get muddled. She could not quit the kitchen for a minute without being afraid she had left the water running, and her fear lest the place should be flooded spoiled all those walks of ours that had once been so happy and free from care.

I thought it odd that my old nurse should be like this, but it did not disturb me, for I did not realize that she would grow worse; but one evening I heard my father and mother talking together in an undertone:

"Mélanie is failing every day, my dear. You can see it."

"She is like a lamp going out for want of oil."

"Do you think it's safe for Pierrot to go about with her out of doors?"

"Ah, my dear Antoinette, she loves the child too well not to have enough strength and intelligence left in her old heart still to take good care of him."

These words came as a revelation to me. I understood—and I wept. The idea that life is fleeting, that it flows by like a stream, then dawned on me for the first time, and from that day forth I clung with wistful eagerness to my old nurse's bony arms and toil-worn hands. I flung my arms about her, but even then she had eluded me.

During that summer, which was a very fine one, her strength improved and her memory came back. She bloomed anew, bustling about round her oven and her saucepans, and I began to tease her again. She went and did her daily shopping, and came back not too much out of breath, and did not find her basket over-heavy. It was like old times again. But when the wet days returned, she complained of feeling giddy. "I'm like a tipsy woman," she used to declare. One day she went out as usual. A little while later there was a ring at the door. It was M. Ménage, who had discovered Mélanie in a fainting fit at the foot of the staircase. She soon came round again and my father said she would get over it that time. I looked at M. Ménage with eager curiosity and studied him with an attentiveness beyond my years, for I had made greater progress in observation than in manners. It was true that M. Ménage had a red, forked beard, that he wore a Rubens hat and breeches *à la hussarde*. But he did not look at all the sort of man to drink blazing punch from a dead man's skull. Laying Mélanie on the sofa, he raised her head and performed the office of the Good Samaritan quite unaffectedly. He seemed gentle and intelligent. With his fine eyes, sad, tender eyes with a hint of weariness in them, he gazed about him in a friendly way, and I thought I saw them light up with a smile as they lingered on my mother's beautiful hair. He looked at me with as much benevolence as a plain child was calculated to inspire, and advised my parents to let Nature, that source of all energy, have her way with me.

M. Ménage was warmly complimented and thanked. My mother was visibly touched by his thoughtfulness in bringing back the basket. Mélanie alone showed no gratitude to the painter for coming to her rescue. He had once gravely offended her by drawing a suppliant Cupid on her bedroom door, and she had never forgiven him for taking such a liberty, so potent is the sense of honour in the bosom of a virtuous woman.

As the doctor had prognosticated, our old servant recovered sufficiently to get about again, but it was clearly time for her to give up work.

There was a deal of whispering behind the scenes, a lot of sighing, wiping away of tears, and tying up of parcels. Covert references were made to one of Mélanie's nieces who had married a farmer named Denisot, and worked a farm with her husband at Jouy-en-Josas.

One morning this niece appeared, humble and grim, a tall, gaunt, swarthy woman. Her teeth were very big, but few in number. She had come to fetch her Aunt Mélanie and to take her away to her home at Jouy. I felt that it was useless to resist, and I burst into tears. We kissed good-bye. To comfort me, my mother promised to take me to Jouy one day soon. Poor old Mélanie was more dead than alive, but I was struck by one profound and subtle thing about her. I saw that when she took off her apron she had severed the ties that had bound her to bourgeois life, and that she was now a person between myself and whom there was no longer any bond of union; she was now, in short, a peasant, and I knew that my beloved Mélanie was lost to me beyond recall.

We went out to see her into the trap in which she was to take her seat beside her niece. A flick of the whip at the mare's ears and off they went. The little white circular crown of her rustic cap looked like a cheese, and I watched it disappear into the distance. That was my first sorrow, and I feel it still.

By losing Mélanie I was losing more than I knew. I was bidding good-bye to the sweetness and joy of my earliest childhood. My mother, who knew Mélanie's worth, was generous enough to feel no jealousy at the love I bore my old nurse, and, if that love was not so great or so august as that which I kept for my mother, it was, perhaps, more tender and assuredly more "intimate."

Mélanie's heart was as simple as my own. It was because there were no sophisticated ideas between us that we were so near to each other. Mélanie was already old when I was born, and she was not given to mirth. That indeed she could not be, for her life had been a hard one, but her shining innocence was to her instead of youth, instead of mirthfulness.

No less, nay more, than my mother herself, Mélanie formed my mode of speech. That, I have no cause to regret. Unlettered as she was, she spoke well.

She spoke well because the words she used were the words that persuade, the words that console. When I tumbled down on the gravel and grazed my knees or the tip of my nose, she spoke healing and comfortable words. If I told her a lie, if I showed selfishness, if I flew into a passion, she would utter the words which bring back to the heart confidence and strength and peace. To her I owe the basis of my moral code, and the additions I have since made thereto are not so firm as that old foundation.

From the lips of my old nurse, I learnt sound

honest French. Mélanie's speech was the speech of
the peasantry, it smacked of the countryside. She
used to say *castrole, ormoire* and *colidor* (instead
of *casserole, armoire,* and *corridor*.) * With that ex-
ception she could have instructed more than one professor, more than one academician, in the art of
speaking. From her lips there flowed the light,
limpid diction of our forefathers. Not knowing
how to read, she pronounced her words as she had
heard them as a child, and they from whom she had
learned them were untutored folk who spoke as
with the voice of Nature herself. And thus it was
that Mélanie's way of talking was both natural and
seemly. Words as rich in colour and as full of

* When educated people like ourselves say *le lierre* for *l'ierre*
and *le lendemain* for *l'en demain*, we ought not to turn up our noses
when we hear common folk talk. Mélanie used to say *une légume*
and *caneçon* for *caleçon;* but just a moment! You find *une légume*
in La Bruyère and *caneçon* is in the *État de la France pour 1692*.
This reminds me of a story which Mélanie once told me, and which
I cannot refrain from setting down here. One day during that
lovely summer which was destined to be the last we were to spend
together, as she was sitting on a seat in the Luxembourg, I fell to
devouring her wrinkled cheeks with kisses. Whereat the dear old
thing, pretending to be alarmed, cried: "Why, are you going to eat
me all up, mon petit monsieur! Have you turned into a were-
wolf?"
    I asked her what a were-wolf was. She didn't answer my
question, but this is the story she told me:
    "In my young days there was a certain boy concerning whom
the report got about at the village inn that he was a wolf and
was destined to eat his mother. The boy, who was simple-minded,
took it seriously. When he returned home that night he went up to
his mother, who had gone to bed, and said to her:
    " 'Mother, my poor mother, I have got to eat you. Give me your
blessing. I am going to devour you . . .' "
    At this point Mélanie stopped short. In vain I urged her to
continue. She would tell me no more. There was this excellent
characteristic about Mélanie's stories—they never ended.

savour as the fruits of our orchards came to her without effort. Her discourse abounded in humorous saws, wise proverbs, and illustrations drawn from the life of field and farmstead.

CHAPTER XXV

RADÉGONDE

T'S a little servant, dear," said my mother to Dr. Nozière, "a little maid from Tours recommended by Madame Caumont. I should rather like you to see her. She has only been in one place before, and that was at an old maiden lady's somewhere near Tours. They say she is thoroughly trustworthy."

And indeed it was high time, for the peace and order of our establishment, that we should get an honest servant from somewhere. During the period —it was rather more than a year—that had elapsed since Mélanie left, we had had a dozen or so of servants, of whom the better ones departed as soon as they found that money was none too plentiful. We had had Sycorax who cultivated a beard on her chin and provided us with nutriment from her witch's cauldron. Then we had a girl of eighteen with a very pretty face. She knew nothing of housework, but my mother thought she would be able to train her. She went off after three days, with half a dozen silver spoons and forks. Next we had some one who had escaped from the Salpêtrière; she said

she was a daughter of Louis Philippe and wore a
string of corks round her neck. And my father—a
member of the faculty—had been the last, dear,
good, simple man, to perceive that she was off her
head. Then there was La Chouette who slept all
day when she ought to have been working, and at
night, when we imagined she was in her attic, ran a
little tavern down at the far end of a court, in the
Rue Mouffetard, where she dispensed the wine she
had stolen from our cellar to a gang of thieves and
vagabonds. For the rest, she was a first-rate cook, a
thorough expert in the art, said my godfather, and
he knew what he was talking about. Hortense Per-
cepied, the last, was, like Penelope, awaiting the
return of her spouse who had gone off to Icaria with
Cabot; she also resembled Penelope in that she
attracted a number of suitors who used to come and
take their meals in the kitchen.

There was the same complaint among the middle
classes in those days as there is now. "You can't
get servants anywhere. Things are not what they
used to be when you could pick up a good, faithful,
steady-going maid without any trouble. Now things
are quite different." Some people blamed the Revolution, which, they said, had put all sorts of high-
falutin notions into the heads of the working-classes
and made them dissatisfied. But when were people
not dissatisfied? The truth of the matter is that
good masters and good servants are rare and always

have been. You don't often come across an Epictetus or a Marcus Aurelius in your journeys up and down the world.

My dear mamma awaited the arrival of the new maid not indeed with a blind confidence, for that was not her way, but certainly not without a favourable presentiment which she was at no pains to conceal. Whence did this arise? It was because she was told that she was a respectable girl, the daughter of honest countryfolk, and that she had been trained in housework by an old maiden lady who belonged to a family of soldiers and magistrates in the provinces; moreover, my mother had it from the Abbé Moinier, her confessor, that it is a great sin to give way to despair.

"What is she called?" asked my father.

"She can be called what you like, dear. She was christened Radégonde."

"I don't care much about the present-day fashion of tampering with servant's names; it seems to me that if you take away the names of members of the human society, you rob them of a part of their personality. Still, I confess Radégonde is rather a mouthful."

When the young girl was announced, my mother did not send me out of the room; this may have been because she forgot to do so (for it was a charming characteristic of hers that she mingled a certain thoughtlessness with the most watchful prudence) or because she thought there was no objection to my taking part in an innocent domestic interview. Radégonde stumped in with big, loud strides. She planted herself in the middle of the drawing-room and stood bolt upright, motionless and mute, her hands folded over her apron, half scared, half defiant. She was very young, little more than a child. She had a florid complexion, and she was neither fair nor dark, neither plain nor good-looking. There was a simple, yet wide-awake look about her which afforded an amusing contrast. She was dressed like the humblest little country girl of her district, but yet not without a certain splendour; her hair was gathered up beneath a lace cap with a great flat top to it, her shoulders were covered with a flower-patterned scarlet shawl. She was very serious and very comic. She took my fancy right away, and I noticed that my parents were not displeased with her. My mother asked her if she could sew. She replied, "Yes, madam." "Cook?" "Yes, madam." "Iron?" "Yes, madam." "Turn out a room?" "Yes, madam." "Do mending?" "Yes, madam."

If my mother had asked her whether she could forge cannon, build cathedrals, compose poems, rule nations, she would still have replied, "Yes, madam," because obviously she said "Yes," without any regard to the meaning of the questions asked her, out of pure politeness, because she thought it was the proper thing, and because her parents had taught

her that it was not good manners to say no to
your superiors:

"Or d'aller lui dire non,*
Sans quelque valable excuse,
Ce n'est pas comme on en use
Avec des divinités."

Thus says La Fontaine who would never have been
able to say no to Mademoiselle de Sillery.

But my mother made no further inquiries regarding the qualifications of the little village maiden. She
told her gently but firmly that she required her to be
neat in appearance and always to be well conducted,
promised to write to her as soon as she had come
to a decision, and dismissed her with the faintest
suspicion of a smile. As she withdrew, little Radégonde somehow or other caught the pocket of her
apron on the door handle. This incident was observed by me alone. I noted every circumstance, and
I was struck with the look of surprise and reproach
which Radégonde gave the offending door knob as
though it had been an evil spirit trying to hold her
captive, as we read in fairy tales.

"What do you think of her, François?" said my
mother.

"She is very young," replied the doctor, "and
then . . ."

Peradventure he may at that moment have caught
a vague and fleeting notion of the genius of Radé-

* Now to go and say no without a valid excuse—that's not the
way to behave with gods and goddesses.

gonde, but it vanished ere he gave it utterance. He did not finish what he was saying. For me, little as I was, and on a level with little things, I had already seen enough to know that this little peasant girl would change our peaceful abode into a haunted house.

"She looks a nice little thing enough," said my mother. "Perhaps I shall be able to train her. If you like, dear, we will call her Justine."

CHAPTER XXVI

CAIRE

E were born on the very same day and at the very same hour and we had grown up together. At first he had answered to the name of Puck, which my father had given him. He was afterwards called Caire, and the change was not to his honour, if honour, that is to say, has anything to do with honesty. Seeing how clever he was at deceit, how cunning a thief, and how rich in rascality, and obliged, withal, to admire the wit and address with which he perpetrated his trickeries, we called him Robert Macaire, after that delightful highwayman in Frédérick Lemaître's play, written fifteen years before—Robert Macaire whom the deft crayon of Honoré Daumier had represented, in the comic papers, successively as a financier, a deputy, a peer of France, and a Minister of State. The name Robert Macaire having been found too long, we had cut it down to Caire. He was a little brown dog of no particular breed but with plenty of brain. That was no wonder; Finette, his mother, used to do her marketing herself, paid the dog's meat man his

money, and brought back her meat to Madame Mathias to be cooked.

Caire's understanding had developed much sooner than mine, and he had long been practising the art of gaining his livelihood when I was still in complete ignorance concerning both the world and myself. As long as I was an infant in arms, he was jealous of me; he never tried to bite me, either because he thought it was too risky or because he looked on me with contempt rather than dislike, but he glowered at my mother and my old nurse with that gloomy and miserable air which betokens envy. A shred of wisdom which this unhappy passion left him prompted him to avoid them, as far as one can avoid people with whom one has to live. He used to run off to my father and spend his days under the doctor's table curled up on a hideous sheepskin mat. As soon as I was able to walk a little, his feelings towards me underwent a change. He became sympathetic and took pleasure in playing with the weakly, tottering little creature. When I was old enough to understand things I admired him. I recognized him as my superior in his profound knowledge of Nature, but in many points I had caught him up.

If Descartes maintained, in complete defiance of probability, that animals are machines, we must excuse him, for he was compelled to do so by his philosophy, and a philosopher always thinks more

of his theories, which are part of himself, than he
does of Nature, which is external, to him.   There
are no Cartesians nowadays, but there may still be
people who will tell you that animals possess instinct and men understanding.   When I was a child
that was the generally professed belief.   It was an
absurdity.   Animals have understanding just as we
have.   It only differs from ours because their organs
are different, and, like ours, it contains the world.
Like animals we possess that secret genius, that unconscious wisdom called instinct, which is far more
precious than the understanding.   Without it neither
flesh, worm, nor Man could survive an instant.

I hold with La Fontaine, who was a better philosopher than Descartes, that animals, particularly in
their wild state, are full of art and ingenuity.   By
taming them we diminish their spirit and cramp their
intelligence.   What capacity for thought would be
left to men supposing them reduced to the condition
to which we reduce dogs and horses, not to mention
the denizens of the poultry yard?   When Zeus suf-
fers a man to fall into bondage, he deprives him of
half his worth.   In fine, whether domesticated or
wild, the creatures of air, earth, and water are one
with us, in that, far down in the depths of their being,
they unite to instinct, which is unerring, reason,
which is fallible.   Like men, they are liable to go
astray.   Caire made mistakes sometimes.

He had a tender affection for Zerbin.   Zerbin

was a spaniel belonging to M. Caumont, the bookseller. A well-brought-up dog. He came of good,
respectable parents, and he loved Caire with a still
greater affection. They were all in all to each other.
Caire's unfortunate reputation had extended to Zerbin, who was now called Zerbin no longer, but Bertrand after Robert Macaire's companion in misdeeds.
Caire led Zerbin astray, and soon made a rogue of
him. Whenever they could slip away unobserved,
they trotted off together, whither heaven only knows,
and came back coated with mud, and limping—ears
torn, eyes bloodshot, but tails up, and happy.

M. Caumont would not let his spaniel have anything to do with our dog. Mélanie, in order to
avoid humiliation and reproaches, made up her mind
that Caire should not cultivate a neighbour of superior lineage and appearance to himself, but friendship is resourceful and laughs at obstacles. In spite
of the watch that was set on them, in spite of bolts
and bars, they discovered countless means of getting
together. Perching himself up on the ledge inside
the dining-room window, which looked on to the
court, Caire sat and waited till his friend should
issue from the bookshop. Bertrand would put himself on view in the court and gaze up with gentle,
pleading eyes at the window whence Caire sat looking affectionately down at him. In spite of every
precaution, they were together in five minutes and
off on all kinds of jaunts and mysterious expedi-

tions. But one day Bertrand, at his customary hour, appeared in the courtyard got up like a sort of miniature lion and looking highly ridiculous. He had been trimmed and clipped by one of those men who in summer-time come and ply their calling at the water's edge down by the Pont Neuf. His coat was ruffled up about his shoulders so as to look like a mane. His hind quarters and his belly had been clipped close. They had a naked, starveling appearance and showed, through his poor shaven skin, a dirty pink colour with dark blue patches here and there. There were little fuzzy tufts round his legs just above the paw, like cuffs, and a tuft, pathetically droll, adorned the tip of his tail. Caire examined him attentively for some time, and then turned away his head; he did not recognize him. Bertrand whined and begged and pleaded; he gazed at him with his lovely, wistful eyes, but all in vain. Caire looked at him no more and sat there waiting.

People say that a dog never laughs. I have seen our Caire laugh, and it was not a pleasant laugh. He laughed a silent laugh, but the tension of his lips and a certain wrinkle in the cheek betokened mockery and sarcasm. One morning I was out shopping with my old nurse. Mouton, the dog belonging to M. Courcelles, the grocer, Mouton, a Newfoundland that could have swallowed Caire at a mouthful, the magnificent Mouton, who was lying stretched out before his master's door, was nonchalantly holding a

leg of mutton bone betwixt his forepaws. Caire in-
spected him for a long time without accosting him
in any way, an omission which, in the dog world,
betrays a lack of good breeding. But Caire didn't
trouble himself much about manners. Mouton, observing the approach of a horse of his acquaintance
that was, as usual, drawing a cartload of Dutch
cheeses, let go his bone and got up to pass the time
of day with his friend. Seizing his opportunity,
Caire slyly picked up the bone between his teeth,
and, taking care not to be seen, made off to hide it at
Simonneau's, the greengrocer's in the Rue des
Beaux-Arts, at whose shop he was a regular visitor.
Then, with an air of assumed unconcern, he returned
in Mouton's direction, looked at him and, seeing that
he was hunting about for his bone, began to laugh.

Caire and I loved each other without being aware
of it, which is a safe and convenient way of loving.
It was about eight years since we had made our joint
appearance on this planet without being quite sure
what we had come there to do, when my poor companion and coeval, who was growing fat and wheezy,
was seized with a painful malady, to wit, stone. He
bore his sufferings uncomplainingly, his coat became
dull and brittle, he grew low-spirited, and would not
eat. The vet performed an operation on him;
but it was not a success. The same evening the
patient ceased to suffer. As he lay in his basket he
turned his fading, friendly eyes towards me, got up,

gave just one wag of his tail, and fell down again.
It was all over with him.   And then I knew how
much he had been to us.   I realized what a power
he had been for us, how he had wrought and thought
and loved and hated; in short, what a great place he
had held in our household and in our thoughts.   I
shed some bitter tears and then fell asleep.   Next
morning I inquired whether Caire's death was in the
paper, like Marshal Soult's.

CHAPTER XXVII

THE DAUGHTER OF THE TROGLODYTES

Y eyes had not deceived me. Radé-
gonde, or I should say Justine—for
my dear mamma had deliberately
transferred her from the patronage
of the noble Thuringian to that of
a saint with a name that came more
trippingly off the tongue—Justine, then, signalized
her arrival by turning our abode into a fairy dwelling place. But do not misconceive me. I do not
mean to say that a fairy godmother had bestowed
on this simple peasant girl the power to deck the
walls of the rooms she cleaned with porphyry, gold,
and precious stones. No. But, since she had entered
upon her duties, our house had become full of weird
noises; there were alarming thuds, panic-stricken
shrieks, gnashing of teeth, and peals of laughter.
The place was filled with the horrible smell of burning fat and charred flesh, water flowed amazingly
about the floor, suddenly there would rise such
clouds of smoke as would turn day into night and
make us gasp for breath; floors creaked, doors
slammed, windows banged, curtains bellied out, the
wind blew in great gusts and there were sinister

portents that brought a cloud to my father's brow;
the ink ran all over his table, his pens lost their
nibs, the chimney of his lamp cracked every night.
Surely this was witchcraft, and no mistake. My
mother kept saying that Justine was not really a
naughty girl, and that with time and patience she
would make a servant of her, but that she broke
rather too much in the process. It was not that
Justine was a clumsy girl. My parents indeed were
often amazed at her dexterity. But she was wild,
headstrong, and, as in her primitive mind she
invested inanimate objects with a soul and imagined
them as being stirred by the same feelings and passions as men and women, this daughter of the Troglodytes of the Loire used to struggle with the kitchen
and household utensils as though with malevolent
beings. She assaulted the hardest metals; window-
catches, and tap-handles fell trophies to her prowess.
In a word, the spirit of her remote forefathers im-
bued her with the most uncouth fetishism. But then
which of us can boast of never having abused some
senseless object which hurt or merely got in our
way—a stone, a splinter, or a twig?

I observed Justine, as she went about her daily
tasks, with a curiosity that never flagged. My
mother upbraided me for what she called my stupid
boobyishness. Therein she misjudged me. Justine
interested me by reason of her fighting spirit and
because all her domestic activities took on the char-

acter of a grim and doubtful conflict. When, brandishing her broom and feather brush, she said in
resolute tones, "I've got to go and do the drawing-
room," I followed eager and expectant, to see what
would come of it.

The drawing-room was furnished with a sofa and
great mahogany armchairs destined to receive, in
their capacious cavities with their shabby red plush
covers, the patients of my father, Dr. Nozière. The
walls were hung with green, striped paper and
adorned with two engravings, *The Dance of the
Hours* and *Napoleon's Dream,* as well as with two
oil paintings cracked all over. They were family
portraits. One was of my grand-uncle and portrayed
a dark complexioned man with a very high coat collar, a white cravat that concealed his chin, and shirt
studs linked with a small gold chain. The
other was a grand-aunt. She wore side curls
and her bust was closely enwrapped in a se-
vere black gown. Both, I was told, were
dressed in the style of Charles X. Painted a
short while before their untimely death, these figures
of a bygone day filled me with a profound melancholy. But what constituted the richest adornment
of this drawing-room were the bronze statuettes presented to my father as a mark of gratitude by patients whom he had cured. Each of these works of
art was an index to the mentality of the donor.
Some were gracious and smiling, others aloof and

austere. There was no similarity between them either in character or workmanship. On one side of the door a little Venus de Milo, cast in chocolate-coloured metal, stood on a small Boule table. On the other, a Flora, in common bronze, was smilingly waving a spray of flowers modelled in gilded zinc. Between two of the windows, bearded and horned, sat the Moses of Michael Angelo; and, here and there, on different tables, were to be seen a young Neapolitan fisherman holding up a crab by one of its claws, a guardian angel flying heavenwards with a little child in his arms, Mignon weeping for her native land, Mephistopheles folding his bat-like wings about him, and Joan of Arc in an attitude of prayer. Finally a Spartacus, who had broken his fetters, stood up fierce and defiant clenching his fists on the clock above the chimney-piece.

To clean them, Justine would violently belabour pictures and bronzes with her stump of a feather broom. This castigation did no appreciable damage to my great uncle or my great aunt, who had already endured manifold hardships, nor did it have any adverse effect on the simple rounded forms of the Venus or the Moses. But the modern sculpture came off badly. Feathers torn violently from the dusting implement got entangled beneath the wings of the guardian angel, between the claws of the crab, underneath Joan of Arc's sword, in Mignon's hair, in Flora's garland, and in the chains of Spartacus.

Justine had no love for these gewgaws, as she called them, and she held the Spartacus in especial detestation. It was he to whom she dealt the rudest buffets. She made him rock on his base. He reeled, he gave a terrible lurch forward as though he would fall on the impious one and crush her as he fell. Then with a fierce frown, the veins standing out on her forehead, she would shout: "Hola! Ho!" as though to the cows she had been wont to bring home from the fields at evening, and finally, with a well directed blow, she would knock him straight on his pedestal again.

In these daily combats, the feather broom soon shed all its plumage. There was only the leather handle and the stick left for Justine to dust with. The treatment soon brought the wings off the guardian angel. Joan of Arc lost her sword, the fisher-lad his crab, Mignon a lock of hair, and Flora had no more flowers left to scatter. Justine did not let that trouble her, but sometimes, as she gazed on the havoc she had wrought, she would stand dreamily, with her hands folded over the broom handle, and murmur with a wistful smile:

"What a pack of duds they are, the lot of them!"

CHAPTER XXVIII

DRAMATIS PERSONÆ

WAS fond of Justine's company. My mother, indeed, thought I was too fond of it. When I come to think over the causes of this predilection, I find several which testify to my innocence and my simplicity. A child's trustfulness, the need for friendship, a love of fun and frolic, and an affectionate disposition, all led me to cultivate her society. But there were other considerations, less to my credit, that drew me to this daughter of the Troglodytes. I thought her rather a simpleton, rather a duffer, and altogether beneath me in intelligence. And so it happened that, when I was in her company, I was often provided with occasions for self-glorification. I greatly enjoyed correcting and instructing her and possibly I was none too indulgent in the process. I was somewhat of a quiz, and she gave me plenty of opportunities for being quizzical. I wanted to be thought much of, so I tried to impress her with my superiority, and held myself up to her as an object of admiration.

I did my best to shine before her, until one day I

found out that, so far from admiring me, she looked on me as quite devoid of sense and judgment, in fact as nothing more or less than a noodle, without a single strong point, in looks or anything else, in my favour. How did I get to know that she harboured sentiments so diametrically opposed to those with which I had credited her? Why, goodness me, because she told me so! Justine was crudely outspoken. She knew how to make herself understood, and I was forced to recognize that she did not admire me in the least. To my credit be it said that I was not angry with her, and that I loved her but little the less in consequence. I diligently inquired into the causes of so unlooked for a judgment, and I succeeded in discovering them, for, whatever the daughter of the Troglodytes might think of me, I was no fool. I will report the result of my researches. To begin with, she beheld me thin, delicate, and pale, not half so sturdy and strong as her brother Symphorien, who was a year younger than I and more of a man. In her idea, a boy ought to have plenty of "go" and determination, to be a dashing, upstanding fellow; and don't for a moment imagine that I disagree with her in that. Then, although it may seem strange that a wench who could not read should hold such a view, she looked on me as an ignoramus. Though she did not say as much, I could see she was astonished that a boy of my age should be unacquainted with

facts about animals and Nature that her brother
Symphorien had known ages ago. My ignorance
on certain subjects struck her as absurd, for
good girl as she was, she was no ninny and had
no respect for simpletons. And then again, although she would sometimes laugh enough to split
her sides, as she would say, she thought it a sign of
a defective understanding to laugh loudly at anything and everything, as I was wont to do. According to her it argued a mistaken view of life, which
is no laughing matter, and a lack of heart. Such
then were the good and solid reasons which led Justine to regard me as devoid of understanding.
And truly they were good enough reasons in themselves, although, as a matter of fact, I was, for a
small boy, capable of taking in a great deal. Sometimes, however, I did behave in a very disconcerting
fashion. Of this I could give a number of instances.
Here at any rate is one which, I fancy, dates back to
Justine's early days in our establishment. On a
what-not in the little room with the rosebud wall-
paper there used to be some little books bound in
green and embellished with illustrations, which my
dear mother sometimes gave me to read. They were
"The Child's Companion." Berquin's stories took
me back to the France of olden times and acquainted
me with manners and customs very different from
those of our day. For example, I read therein the
story of a young nobleman of ten who wore a sword

which he was too fond of drawing on the little village children with whom he chanced to quarrel. But one day, instead of a blade, he drew from the sheath a peacock's feather which his wise tutor had put there instead. Picture to yourself his shame and confusion. The lesson did him good. After that he was never arrogant and quarrelsome. To me these tales had a certain element of freshness about them; they moved me to tears. One morning I remember reading the tale of two gendarmes who greatly touched me by their kindness and devotion. They used to go about bringing happiness into the lives of poor peasant folk—how they did it I have forgotten—and the peasants invited them to supper. As there were no plates in the cottage, the good gendarmes ate their stew on their bread. That struck me as such a fine thing that I made up my mind to copy them at luncheon. Despite my mother's very justifiable protests, I insisted on putting my haricot mutton on my bread. I spilt the gravy all down my clothes, my mother scolded me and Justine looked at me with compassion.

The incident was a slight one. It reminds me of another one of a similar nature, not less trivial. All the same I am going to relate it, for it is not greatness that is important to my subject, but truth.

I read Berquin; I also read Bouilly. More modern than Berquin, Bouilly was not less touching. To him I owe my acquaintance with one Lise who sent

her pet sparrow to Madame Helvétius with mes-
sages soliciting her favour on behalf of a family that
had fallen on evil days. I conceived a deep, nay, a
violent affection for Lise. I asked my mother
whether she were still alive. My mother replied
that she would be very old if she were. I next became enamoured of a little orphan of whom M.
Bouilly drew a delightful portrait. He was a poor
little boy without shelter and half naked. An old
scholar took him in and made him work in his li-
brary. He gave him his old clothes to wear, nice
warm things, which had to be altered a little to make
them fit. That is the part I liked best in the story.
I longed for nothing so much as to be dressed like
Bouilly's little orphan boy, in a man's old clothes. I
asked my father and my godfather for theirs, but
they only made fun of me. One day, when I was at
home alone, I lighted in the depths of a cupboard
on a frock-coat that seemed to have seen its best
days. I put it on and went to look at myself in the
glass. It trailed on the ground and the sleeves
came down over my hands. So far, there was no
great harm done, but, in order, I fancy, to conform
to the story in all its details, I curtailed the coat
a little with the scissors. The consequence was that
I found myself with a very awkward piece of business on hand. Aunt Chausson went out of her way
on this occasion to credit me with perverted instincts;
my mother rebuked me for what she inappropriately

termed my mischievous monkey-tricks. I was misunderstood. What I wanted was to be a gendarme *à la Berquin*, an orphan *à la Bouilly*, to play a variety of characters, to live several lives. I was giving vent to a burning desire to get out of myself, to be some one else, several other persons, every other person, had that been possible, all humanity, the whole natural world; whereof there only remains with me the rather unusual faculty of entering into other people's points of view, of forming a good, occasionally a too good, estimate of the arguments and opinions of my opponents. It was this latter trait that convinced Justine beyond all manner of doubt that I was not right in my head. In fact, she soon came to look on me as a dangerous idiot.

When I came to learn the stories of the Crusades, the lofty exploits of the Christian barons fired me with enthusiasm. It is good to imitate the things you admire. In order to be as much as possible like Godefroy de Bouillon, I fashioned myself a suit of armour and a helmet out of some cardboard on which I had gummed pieces of the silver paper that chocolates are wrapped in. To critics who point out that such a suit was more like the burnished armour of the fifteenth century than the coats of mail of the twelfth and thirteenth, I would deliberately reply that more than one illustrious painter has been guilty of far more serious liberties in this respect. At all events, the really essential part of my outfit consisted, as will presently but too plainly appear, in a double-bladed axe cut out of cardboard and fixed on to the end of an old sunshade handle.

The kitchen represented Jerusalem, and I took it by storm. I also belaboured Justine who, while lighting the kitchen fire, had to be an infidel, much against her will. The faith that clothed me like a robe of fire lent might to my arm. Justine was not made of cotton wool, she was indeed, as she herself was wont to remark, "a tough 'un," and she would have endured the onslaught of the two-bladed axe with equanimity had it not become entangled with her cap. Now this cap of hers she looked upon as something beyond all price, not only because of its pleasing shape and its valuable lace, but for reasons of a deeper and more mysterious import—because it was, perhaps, for her an emblem of her native place, a symbol of her country, the insignia of the daughters of the land she loved. She looked on it as something august, something sacred. And, now, behold her bereft of it in most ignoble fashion. She heard it give. But with the same blow I had done worse still: I had disarranged Justine's chignon.

With the virgin shyness of some timid wild creature she would not suffer anything, not even a mother's hand, not even a breath of air, to interfere with the arrangement of her hair, which with its narrow plaits patted tightly down was unbecoming enough in all conscience. Never on any occasion had she been discovered with her hair down, not even during an illness which kept her six weeks in bed in her own room, when my mother went every day to make her comfortable; not even on that night of terror when some one shouted "Fire" and the concierge saw her rushing across the court with bare feet, in her night-dress, her hair in the most perfect order. To preserve this unvarying mode of coiffure was for her a matter of honour, of glory, nay of conscience. A single hair out of place would have been a disgrace. As she felt these blows raining down on her cap and headgear, Justine shook all over and put her hands to her head. She was loath to believe the full extent of her misfortune. She was obliged to feel about the nape of her neck three times before she could convince herself that her cap had been battered in and her coiffure profaned. But the evidence was too horribly convincing. There was a hole in the lace big enough to put your finger through, and a wisp of hair about as long and as thick as a rat's tail was hanging down her back. Thereupon the heart of Justine was filled with an exceeding bitter sorrow.

"I shan't stop any longer," she cried in doleful tones.

She asked no redress, for the outrage was irreparable, and without wasting words in vain reproaches, without so much as a glance in my direction, she went out of the kitchen. My mother had all the difficulty in the world to get her to change her mind. There is no doubt that the daughter of the Troglodytes would never have resumed her apron if, on reflexion, she had not come to the conclusion that her young master was more of a fool than a knave.

CHAPTER XXIX

MADEMOISELLE MÉRELLE

N those days, if I mistake not, there was a gentleness about life, a certain air of good fellowship about men and things, an atmosphere of intimate and gracious charm that to-day exists no longer. It seems to me as though people were nearer to one another then, or, perhaps, it was because I was a child and tender-hearted, that they seemed to be more closely united one to another. Be that as it may, you might have seen many a morning, in the courtyard of the house where I was born, M. Bellaguet, in his Turkish cap and check dressing-gown, having a friendly chat with M. Morin, who was the concierge next door and an employé at the Chamber of Deputies. Whoever did not see them thus, missed a fine sight, for the pair of them typified, as it were, the regime inaugurated by the *Trois Glorieuses*. However, the misfortune is not irremediable, for you may get the two characters repeated a hundred times over in Daumier's lithographs. In short, everybody knew everybody else in those days, and when three o'clock in the af-

ternoon came round and my mother was sitting at
the window sewing, with a pot of mignonette in front
of her, she would exclaim, as she glanced down at
the glass roof above the steps:

"There's Mademoiselle Mérelle going to give
her grammar lesson to M. Bellaguet's little girl.
Mademoiselle Mérelle is charming, and her manners are so nice."

It was generally held that Mademoiselle Mérelle
was a lady and that she always dressed in good taste.
If I was haphazard, in describing her dress, I
should depict her for you in the fashion of the
present day. I believe it is always the way. As
time goes on we re-array the young women we
used to know in clothes of the latest mode. It is the
same thing on the stage with plays that have seen
ten, fifteen, or twenty years go by. Every time
they are revived, the heroine's gowns are brought
up to date. But I have the historic sense and a liking for the things of old. I shall, therefore, carefully eschew those modernizing practices that change
the physiognomy of an epoch, and so I here put it
on record that Mademoiselle Mérelle, then about
twenty-six or twenty-seven, wore leg of mutton
sleeves, and that her skirt, unlike those of the present day, grew wider as it went down. She wore a
cashmere scarf wrapped tightly across her chest, and
she had, as the saying went, a wasp-like waist. I
nearly forgot to say that long side curls adorned her

cheeks with their golden ringlets, and that she wore according to the season a bonnet of velvet or Leghorn, a poke bonnet, which projected so far forward as completely to conceal her profile. To put it briefly, she was the last word in fashion.

Now, at the time of which I am speaking, I was eight years old. My stock of knowledge was scanty, but it came from a good source. It was my mother who had imparted it to me. It included reading, writing and arithmetic. I wrote and spelt pretty well for my age, so they said, except for the participles. My mother as a child had conceived a mortal dread of participles. She had never got over it, and she took good care not to lead me into grammatical mazes in which she was apprehensive that she herself might lose her way. My mother, dear soul, was the only one of them all who credited me with brains. Every one else, including my father and my nurse, looked on me as rather an ordinary child, intelligent enough in a way, but not the way of other children. I was of a more speculative turn, and, being occupied with things of more varied range and greater diversity, my mind seemed less compact and less collected than theirs. My parents thought me too young and too delicate to go to boarding school, and they had no very high opinion of the little academies round about, which they rightly considered as dirty and ill-managed. My father came home with a specially bad impression of an establishment in the Rue des Marais-Saint-Germain which he had been to see. At the far end of a dirty, stuffy room sat an apoplectic dominie puffing and panting with corpulence and choler. He had some dozen ur-chins, all wearing dunce's caps, kneeling in front of his chair, and he was threatening the rest of the class with the birch—thirty little ragamuffins who, laughing, crying, and yelling all together, were en-gaged in throwing their inkpots, their satchels, and their books at each others' heads.

In these circumstances, my mother conceived the idea of getting Mademoiselle Mérelle to act as my governess—the celebrated Mademoiselle Pauline Mérelle herself. The enterprise was ambitious and fraught with considerable difficulty. Mademoiselle Mérelle only taught in the houses of the nobility or of such middle-class families as were rolling in money. They had to be either rich or titled people. She was the protégée of old Bellaguet, our landlord, who had married one of his daughters to a Vil-leragues and another to a Monsaigle, and there were doubts as to whether she would consent to teach the son of an obscure little local doctor. For my father was poor, and his rooted dislike to ac-cepting fees was not calculated to make him rich, to say nothing of the fact that, being of a meditative disposition, he spent, in reflecting on the destiny of humankind, valuable hours which, had he been less of a genius, he would have devoted to looking after his worldly affairs. Thus Dr. Nozière was rich only in sentiments and ideas. My mother, who was nevertheless anxious to have me taught by Mademoiselle Mérelle, persuaded Madame Montet, the cashier at the Petit-Saint-Thomas, to say a word to her. Madame Montet was a patient of my father's, and was said to be a great friend of Mademoiselle Mérelle's mother. The latter was a great churchgoer, was everlastingly to be seen carrying a horse-hair reticule, and looked more like her daughter's maid than her mother. So, at least, I have heard, for I never saw her myself.

Through the good offices of Madame Montet, the young governess consented to take me every day, from one to two o'clock.

"Pierre, Mademoiselle Mérelle will give you your first lesson to-morrow," said my mother, with a restrained joy, in which a note of pride could be detected.

On hearing this I went to bed in such a state of excitement that it was at least ten mintues before I fell asleep, and I believe I dreamt about it.

Next morning, my mother made me dress with greater care than usual. She put pomade on my hair and parted it herself, and I put on more pomade on my own account, after she had gone. I should have washed my hands again had I not known from experience that it was useless and that, do what one will, little boys' hands are never anything but dirty.

Mademoiselle Mérelle came at the appointed hour. She came, and lo, all the rooms were pervaded with the scent of heliotrope! My mother conducted us both into the little room with the rosebud wall paper, next to her own. She installed us at a little mahogany side table and, having promised that no one should disturb us, she withdrew.

Forthwith Mademoiselle Mérelle unfastened a dainty little Russia leather writing-case, took from it a sheet of notepaper and a pen-holder made of a porcupine quill with a silver knob at the end, and began to write. She wrote very rapidly and only paused now and then to look up at the ceiling and smile, and to tell me to read La Fontaine's fables, which happened to be lying on the table. In this manner we got through the first lesson, and when my mother asked me if Mademoiselle Mérelle had made me work hard I said yes, without quite realizing that I was not exactly telling the truth.

The following day, when we had again seated ourselves at the little table, my governess once more told me to get on with a fable what time she herself continued writing in a sort of seraphic rapture. Sometimes she stopped as though waiting for an inspiration, and, whenever by chance her gaze rested on me, her expression betokened mild and tranquil indifference. The third lesson passed off in the same manner, and so did those which followed. I sat and feasted my eyes upon her. During the three-

quarters of an hour that the lesson lasted, I drank
in the light of her eyes. To me those eyes of hers
seemed a wondrous marvel, and even now, after all
these years, a marvel I still believe they were. They
seemed as though fashioned of Parma violets. Long
lashes lent them mystery and shadow. No detail of
that pretty face have I forgotten. Mademoiselle
Mérelle's nostrils were rather wide apart, pink inside, like a kitten's; her mouth curved upwards a little at the corners, and there was a slight down on her
lip whereof my juvenile organs of vision, magnify-
ing like a lens, seemed to distinguish each infinites-
imal separate hair. The leisure thus bestowed on
me by my governess was employed, not in reading
La Fontaine's fables, as she recommended me, but in
contemplating her and in wondering to myself what
manner of letters she could be writing; and I was
convinced that they were love-letters. Therein I was
right, save that at that time Mademoiselle Mérelle's
ideas and mine, regarding the nature of love, did not
precisely coincide. Having further speculated as
to who the people were to whom she used to write,
I conjectured that they must be angels in Paradise,
not that the supposition seemed very probable even
in my own eyes, but it spared me the pangs of jealousy.

Mademoiselle Mérelle never spoke a word to
me. I heard the sound of her voice when she read
over some of the phrases she had written, some-

times in tones of gentle melancholy, sometimes of
sparkling glee.   I was unable to catch their meaning.   I remember, however, that she used to speak
of flowers and birds, of the stars, and the ivy which
dies on that round which it winds its tendrils.   The
tones of her voice awoke responsive music in my
heart.

Now my mother's awe concerning participles was
really nothing more nor less than superstition. From
time to time she would inquire whether we had
reached that part of the grammar, as in her view it
was the most puzzling and difficult of all, particularly the distinction between the verbal adjective
and the present participle. I replied vaguely and in
such terms that she worried herself with the thought
that perhaps I was not quite so bright as I might have
been.   But how was I to tell her that all I took in
from Mademoiselle Mérelle were her eyes, her lips,
her fair hair, her perfume, her gentle breathing, the
soft rustle of her dress, and the sound of her pen as
it sped over the paper.

I never grew tired of gazing at my governess, but
I admired her most of all when, pausing in her writing, a wistful look came into her eyes, and she would
sit, deep in thought, with the silver ball of her pen-
holder resting on her nether lip.   In after years,
when I saw—in the Museum at Naples—that picture from Pompeii which portrays, in the form of a
medallion, a poetess, a Muse with her style resting

on her lip in precisely the same manner, I felt a thrill as I thought of those delicious hours of childhood.*

Yes, I loved Mademoiselle Mérelle, and what made her nearly as adorable in my eyes as her beauty was her indifference, her infinite and divine indifference. My governess never spoke a word to me, never vouchsafed me a smile; never bestowed on me a word of praise or blame. Perhaps, if she had shown the least symptom of kindness the spell would have been broken. But during the ten months that I had lessons with her, she never displayed the smallest interest in me. Sometimes, with the innocent audacity of my age, I attempted to kiss her; I stroked her rich dress, glossy as a bird's plumage, I endeavoured to sit on her knee. She just put me aside as though I had been a puppy, with never so much as a reproachful or warning word. And so, feeling she was inaccessible, I rarely indulged in such manifestations. Nearly all the time I was in her company, I was in a condition bordering on idiocy and sunk deep in a state of gaping beatitude. When I was but eight years old I made proof that he is the happy man who, having abandoned mental effort and the attempt to arrive at an intellectual understanding of things, loses himself in the contem-

---

* Without doubt she was a Muse. But in the same museum there is another Pompeian painting representing the wife of Proculus, the baker, with her style in the same position and her household account book.

plation of the beautiful; and it was revealed to me
that unbounded desire, desire that knows neither
fear nor hope, desire that is unconscious of its own
existence, brings to the mind and to the senses the
very consummation of happiness, for it is unto itself
entire contentment and its own complete satisfaction.
But that is a truth that I had quite forgotten by the
time I was eighteen, and I have never been able
thoroughly to recapture it since. I used then to
remain stock still in contemplation of her, my fists
dug well into my cheeks, and my eyes wide open with
wonder. When at length I awoke from my trance
(for after all I did awake from it) I gave evidence
of this reawakening of mind and body by kicking
the table and making blots on the fables of La
Fontaine. But it only needed a look from Mademoiselle Mérelle to plunge me once again into a condition of beatific coma. That look of hers, devoid
alike of love and hate, was always enough to deprive
me of sense and motion.

When she departed, I used to go down on my
knees in front of her chair. It was a little ebony
chair in the style of Louis Philippe, intended to look
like Gothic. The back was shaped like a pointed
arch. The seat was upholstered in fine tapestry and
represented a spaniel on a red cushion, and this chair
I looked on as the most beautiful thing in the world
when Mademoiselle Mérelle was seated on it. But,
truth to tell, my meditations used not to last long,

and I turned from the rosebud-papered study, skipping and jumping and shouting at the top of my voice. My mother told me that I was never so noisy as in those days, and it is a family tradition that I used to run Justine very close in the production of disasters. While the little maid was out in the kitchen smashing up the crockery, I set fire to the green lamp-shade with the Chinese figures on it, which my father thought so much of and which had been with us so long that it had come to be looked on as immortal. Sometimes we were partners, Justine and I, in the same cataclysm, as happened on the day when, each holding a bottle, we fell from top to bottom of the cellar stairs, and again on that tragic morning when, being both engaged in watering the flowers on the window ledge, we dropped the watering pot right on to M. Bellaguet's head. It was at this period, too, that my passion for lead soldiers was at its height. I used eagerly to arrange them in order of battle on the dining-room table, and there I fought the most terrible battles despite the remonstrances of Justine, anxious perhaps to lay the cloth, who, when I persisted in my refusal to pack away my fighting men in their boxes, would, despite my clamorous protests, sweep them all off, victors and vanquished alike, into her apron. To pay her out I hid her work-box in the oven, and did my level best to bedevil the guileless creature. In a word I was a genuine boy, the real unadulterated

article, a merry restless little animal up to any piece
of mischief. It is, nevertheless, true that Mademoiselle Mérelle exercised an irresistible power over
me, and that the sight of her acted upon me like one
of those magic spells we read of in Eastern tales of
mystery.

Now it came to pass that one day at dinner, after
ten months of this enchanted existence, my mother
informed me that my governess was not coming any
more.

"Mademoiselle Mérelle," went on my mother,
"told me to-day that you had made sufficient progress to go to school after the holidays."

The marvel is that I received this news without
amazement, without despair, almost without regret.
It did not surprise me. On the contrary, it seemed
natural that the apparition should, after the manner
of apparitions, fade away. This, at any rate, is the
only explanation I can offer of my imperturbability.
Mademoiselle Mérelle was already so remote from
my sphere, even when she was with me, that I was
able to endure the thought of her going away altogether. And, besides, little boys of eight have no
great faculty for sustained feelings of suffering and
regret.

"Thanks to your governess's tuition," pursued my
mother, "you now know enough French grammar to
go straight into the second form. I feel truly grateful to that charming young woman for teaching you

the rules about participles. They are the most difficult part of speech in our language, and unfortunately I was never able to master them, for I was
never properly grounded."

My dear mother was labouring under a delusion.
No, Mademoiselle Mérelle did not teach me the participles, but she revealed to me truths still more
precious, secrets still more valuable. She initiated
me into the cult of all things gracious and comely;
by her indifference she taught me to love beauty even
when it was unresponsive and remote, to love it
with detachment, an art that is sometimes necessary
in this life.

I ought to let Mademoiselle Mérelle's story conclude there. I know not what evil spirit it is that
compels me to spoil the ending. Anyhow, I won't
waste words in doing so. Mademoiselle Mérelle
did not remain a governess. She went to live on
Lake Como with young Villeragues, who did not
marry her himself. He married her instead to his
uncle Monsaigle, so that in this respect her destiny
resembled Lady Hamilton's. But it flowed in ob-
scurer and more tranquil channels. I had several
opportunities of seeing her again, but I studiously
avoided them.

CHAPTER XXX

DIVINE MADNESS

BOUT this time, at the close of a fine summer's day, I was seated near the window turning over the leaves of my picture Bible. It was very old and very tattered, and the engravings being in a hard pompous style, though they sometimes excited my surprise, did not charm me, for they lacked that gentleness without which nothing ever gave me pleasure. There was only one picture which I liked, and that was of a lady wearing a very small head-dress, her hair flat and smooth on the crown of her head, puffed out over the ears, and done up behind in the form of a ball. She was very daintily decked out in the style of Louis XIII. She wore a lace collar and, standing on an Italian terrace, was offering a tall beaker filled with water to Jesus Christ. I was contemplating this dame who seemed beautiful to me; I was meditating upon the mysterious scene, and above all I was admiring the beaker because of its graceful contour and the diamond points which adorned its foot. And I was full of the desire to possess such a glass when my mother called me and said:

"Pierre, to-morrow we will go and see Mélanie. That will please you, I expect?"

Yes, I was pleased. It was now more than two years since Mélanie had left us to go and live in retirement with her niece, the wife of a farmer at Jouy-en-Josas. At first I had fervently longed to see my old nurse, and I begged and prayed my dear mamma to take me to her. As time went on my longing began to diminish, and now I had grown used to not seeing her, and the memory of her, already remote, was dimmer in my heart. Yes, certainly I was pleased, but, truth to tell, it was the thought of the journey that pleased me most. With my old Bible open on my knees, I fell to thinking of Mélanie and reproaching myself for my ingratitude. I strove to love her as I had used to do. I drew the picture of her from the deeps of my heart where it lay inurned. I rubbed it up and burnished it, and managed to impart to it the aspect of something a little the worse for wear perhaps, but, nevertheless, clean and well cared for.

At dinner, seeing my mother drinking out of a commonish sort of glass, I said:

"Mamma, when I am grown up I will give you a beautiful glass as tall as a flower vase with a tapering stem, like the one I saw in an old engraving which represents a lady handing a glass of water to Jesus Christ."

"I take the will for the deed, Pierre," said my

mother, "but we have got to think about taking a
cake for poor old Mélanie, who is so fond of sweet
things."

We went by train to Versailles; when we arrived
at the station we found a covered cart waiting for
us. It was drawn by a lame horse and driven by a
lad with a wooden leg. We drove to Jouy across
a valley with streamlets winding through meadows
and orchards, and shadowy woods crowning the
summits of the hills.

"This is a pretty road," said my mother. "No
doubt it was still prettier in the spring when the
pears, cherries and peaches were all in blossom,
bouquets of white, warmed and brightened with pink.
But then only pale, shy flowers would have been
found among the grass, crowfoot and meadow dais-
ies. The summer flowers are bolder; rose campion,
cornflowers, larkspur, poppies; see how they flash
their colours back at the sun!"

I was delighted with everything I saw. We arrived at the farm and found Madame Denizot in
the yard, standing by a manure heap with a stable
fork in her hand.

She ushered us into the smoke blackened kitchen
where Mélanie, seated at the chimney corner in a
tall wooden arm-chair, roughly padded with straw,
was knitting with blue coloured wool. A swarm of
flies buzzed and circled about her. A saucepan
hummed a tune on the hearth. As we came in,

Mélanie made an effort to rise. My mother put her arm about her affectionately, and made her keep her seat. We exchanged kisses. My lips sank into her soft cheeks. She moved her lips, but no words came.

"Poor old soul," said Madame Denizot, "she's got out of the way of talking. It's not to be wondered at, she has very little call to do any talking here."

Mélanie wiped her misty eyes with a corner of her apron. She smiled on us and her tongue was loosened:

"Gracious goodness, and can it be you, Madame Nozière? You haven't altered, and how your little Pierre has grown; grown out of all knowledge! The dear child is pushing us into the next world."

She asked for my father, such a fine looking man and so kind to poor folk; for my Aunt Chausson, who used to pick up pins when she saw them on the floor, and quite right, too, for we ought not to let anything get lost; for kind Madame Laroque, who used to make me jam sandwiches, and for Navarino, her parrot, who once gave me such a nip that the blood flowed. She inquired whether my godfather, M. Danquin, still liked trout cooked in wine as much as ever, and if Madame Caumont had found a husband for her eldest daughter. While she was asking all these questions, without waiting for them to be answered, Mélanie had picked up her knitting again.

"What's that you're making, Mélanie?" asked my mother.

"A woollen petticoat for my niece."

"She keeps dropping stitches and never picks them up," said the niece, with a shrug and without lowering her voice. "She keeps getting it narrower and narrower. It's wool thrown away."

M. Denizot, having taken off his working boots, now came in and saluted the company.

"Madame Nozière," said he, "you may be sure the old soul wants for nothing."

"She costs us a pretty penny," added Madame Denizot.

I watched her as she knitted her petticoat, a little grieved for her sake that it was wool thrown away. She had only one glass in her spectacles, and that was cracked in three pieces. This, however, did not seem to trouble her.

We chatted like old friends, but we had not a great deal to say to each other. She was overflowing with maxims, and instilled into me that one should respect one's father and mother, never waste a piece of bread, and learn what was necessary to play one's part in life. All this bored me. Giving a turn to the conversation, I told her that the elephant was dead and that a rhinoceros had come to the Jardin des Plantes.

Thereupon she began to laugh and said:

"I can't help laughing when I think of Madame Sainte-Lucie at whose house I used to be in service when I was a young girl. One day she went to see the rhinoceros at the fair, and asked a fat man dressed up like a Turk whether he was the rhinoceros. 'No, madame,' answered the fat man, 'I'm the man what shows it.' "

She next spoke—I don't remember what brought it up—of the Cossacks who came to France in 1815. And she told me over again the story she had told me times without number, during our walks in the old days.

"One of those blackguardly Cossacks tried to kiss me. I wouldn't let him, and nothing in this world would have made me do it. My sister Célestine told me to be careful as they had the upper hand of us, and that if I rebuffed them like that they might set fire to the village out of spite. And in fact they were a vindictive lot. All the same I didn't let myself be kissed."

"Mélanie, would you have pushed away the Cossack like that if you had been sure that he would set fire to the village if you did?"

"I would have pushed him away if my father and mother, my uncles, aunts, nephews, nieces, brothers and sisters, Monsieur le Maire, Monsieur le Curé, and all the people had been burnt in their houses, and all the cattle and all the stock into the bargain."

"They were very ugly, weren't they, Mélanie, those Cossacks?"

"Oh, yes! They had flat noses, slit eyes, and goat beards. But they were tall and strong, and the one who wanted to kiss me was a fine specimen of his tribe, a big strapping fellow. He was one of the leaders."

"And they were very wicked men, the Cossacks?"

"Oh, yes! If any harm came to one of their number, they would lay waste the whole country round with fire and sword. People used to go and hide in the woods. The Cossacks were always saying *Capout,* and made signs that they would cut off our heads. We had to be very careful not to thwart them when they had been drinking brandy, for then they used to go raving mad, and struck at every one within reach, regardless of age or sex. When they were short of victuals they shed tears at having left their country, and some few among them used to perform on an instrument like a small guitar and played such melancholy tunes that it nearly broke your heart to listen to them. My cousin, Niclausse, killed one of them and threw the body into a well, but no one got to know of it. We put up a dozen of them at the farm. They drew water, carried wood, and minded the children."

I had heard these tales many and many a time.
They always interested me.

While we were alone with Mélanie, my mother
slipped a little piece of gold into her hand, and I
saw the poor old thing tremble as she clutched it and
she hid it in her apron with such an expression of
greed and fear as it pained me to behold. Was this
then that same Mélanie who used to take pennies out
of her own pocket, unknown to my mother, in order
to buy me sweets?

However, the old soul regained her equanimity,
and resumed her flow of talk. Smilingly she recalled the pranks I used to play her. She told how
I drove her nearly crazy by putting her brooms
where she could not find them, or by concealing heavy
weights in her basket when she was getting ready to
go shopping. She was merry and seemed to have
thrown off the weight of years. At this point it came
into my head to say:

"And your saucepans, Mélanie, the saucepans
which you kept so bright and which you thought so
much of?"

As she thought of them Mélanie sighed deeply
and big tears coursed down her wrinkled cheeks.

The table was laid for my mother and me in the
bedroom, which smelt of linen freshly washed. The
walls were whitewashed, and, ranged along by the
looking-glass on the mantelpiece, were a couple of
daguerreotypes of Monsieur and Madame Denizot,

and an old fencing master's diploma festooned with tricolour flags. I wanted them to let my old nurse come and have her lunch with us. But the farmer's wife said that her aunt had lost all her teeth, that she ate very slowly, that she was accustomed to have her meals in the kitchen by herself, and that if we had her beside us at table she would not feel at her ease.

I made a very good lunch, a savoury omelet, the wing of a chicken and a piece of cheese. I drank a nip of new wine, and my mother bade me go and take a look round the farm.

The sun was beginning its downward course and was breaking its spears of fire upon the peaceful foliage of the trees. Thin, white clouds hung motionless in the heavens. Larks were singing low down over the fields. A strange light-heartedness took possession of my soul. The influence of Nature stole in upon my being through the portal of every sense, and a delicious eagerness set me all aglow. I shouted, I bounded along beneath the lofty trees, I was drunk, visited with that frenzy which I recognized later on when I came to read those Greek poets who sang of the dances of the Mænads. Like them I danced, and, dancing, waved a thyrsus torn from a stripling hazel. Trampling on grass and flowers, inebriated with the fresh air and the scent of the woods and fields, whipped by yielding twigs, I sped along like a wild thing.

My mother called me and pressed me to her bosom.

"Pierrot," she said, with a trace of anxiety in her voice, "you're in a bath of perspiration. How hot your forehead is, and how your heart is beating!"

CHAPTER XXXI

ELL, at all events," said my mother,
"he can't always be left to moon
about from morning till night with
Justine."

"Reading whatever he happens
to lay hands on," said my father.
Yesterday I discovered him deep in a treatise on
obstetrics."

They decided to send me to school.

After a great deal of looking about, my father
found a place to suit me, an educational establishment under clerical control, and attended by the sons
of gentlemen. These were two essentials in the
eyes of my parents, who had leanings towards religion and the aristocracy. Not wishing to part with
their only son, they did not make a boarder of me,
and for that I entertain feelings of gratitude towards
them that will cease only with my life. However, to
send me to school for two hours in the morning
and then again for two hours in the afternoon they
deemed neither possible nor desirable. My mother
was suffering at that time from heart trouble, and
Justine, having all the cooking and housework on

her hands, really had not the time to go backwards
and forwards twice a day to take me all the way to
school. They were also afraid that, without the
master's eye upon me, I might be tempted to scamp
my homework. The apprehension was not without
foundation, for I should not have been very eager to
devote myself to improving my mind with study,
what time Justine was in her kitchen making ready
to enact her flood-and-fire performance, or doing
battle in the dining-room with Moses and Spartacus.
In order that I might not be cut off from my own
folk, and also that I might be subjected to the necessary discipline, I was sent as a day-boarder. Justine
had to make it her business to take me to St. Joseph's
at eight o'clock in the morning and fetch me again
at four in the afternoon.

St. Joseph's school was housed in a mansion in
the Rue Bonaparte, an old building with an aristocratic air about it.

I will not go so far as to say that I took in the
beauty of its style, or that I appreciated, at its due
worth, the noble stone staircase with its wrought iron
balusters, and the great rooms whose whiteness was
tempered by the shadowy green reflected from the
trees without, the rooms in which M. Grépinet held
his classes. My uncultured taste rather prompted
me to admire the chapel with its coloured statue of
the Virgin, its vases of paper flowers under their

glass globes, and its gilt lamp suspended from a blue star-spangled firmament.

As this establishment was a preparatory school for the College X. it was not like the *lycées* where the little boys are victimized by the big ones after the manner of minnows and pike in lakes and rivers. Being all very young, all equally strengthless, and as yet but little advanced in iniquity, we did not unduly tyrannize over one another. The masters were mild-mannered men; the childish simplicity of the ushers was a bond between ourselves and them. In short, though I did not greatly enjoy myself in this house, I was not a prey to those fits of sadness that were destined, later on, to cast a gloom over my school life. Opining that Mademoiselle Mérelle had taught me enough French, they enrolled me in the second form and—though I never learned the reason why—put me with the boys who knew a certain amount of grammar and had been through the *Epitome*. But, then, is it always so easy to find out why the authorities act as they do, whether in public or in private matters? In the days when I passed under the ferule of M. Grépinet, there flourished a philosopher with a kindly eye and long drooping moustaches whose name was Victor Considérant. I had seen him scores of times fishing with a line beneath the Pont Royal, and he was then giving out to the world, on the authority of Fourier, his master, that

mankind would enjoy the benefits of a good government, when they found themselves in harmony, that
is to say, in a state regulated in every detail by Victor Considérant himself. When that time comes,
no little animal as ignorant as I was will
be put into M. Grépinet's class, and the condition of the human race will be ameliorated in
many other respects. We shall only do what we
have a mind to do. Like the baboons we shall have
a tail wherewith to suspend ourselves from the trees,
and an eye at the tip of that tail. This at any rate
was the account my godfather used to give of the
phalansterian philosophy. Meantime, things go on
pretty much as they used to in my young days, and,
taking them all round, schoolboys fare no better and
no worse than little Pierre Nozière.

My master, then, was called Grépinet. I
see him now, as he sat there in front of me.
Endowed by nature with a big nose and a
thick drooping underlip, he resembled Lorenzo
di Medici, not on account of the laxity of
his morals but the ugliness of his features. This
was borne in upon me when I saw the medals of
Lorenzo the Magnificent. If medals of M. Grépinet were obtainable, the only difference between
them and Lorenzo's would be the price we should
have to pay for them. The likenesses would be
the same. M. Grépinet was a very worthy man, unless I am greatly mistaken, and an excellent form-

master. It was assuredly not his fault that I derived small profit from his lessons. The first one
enchanted me. As I listened to the voice of M.
Grépinet, I beheld visions of delight rise up as if
by magic from a book that to me was more unde-
cipherable than the most recondite of hieroglyphics.
It was the *De Viris*. A shepherd discovered, among
the reeds of the Tiber, a pair of new-born babes to
whom a she-wolf was giving suck. He bore them to
his hut, where his wife took charge of them and
brought them up as shepherd boys, unwitting that
the blood of gods and kings flowed in their veins.
I beheld them all as, one after another, the master's
voice summoned them forth from the dim recesses
of the text, all those heroes of the wondrous tale,
Numitor and Amulius, kings of Alba Longa, Rhea
Silvia, Faustulus, Acca Laurentia, Romulus and
Remus. I was occupied, heart and soul, with the
story of their adventures. The music of their names
rendered them beautiful in my sight. When Justine
came to take me home, I told her all about the twins
and the she-wolf which suckled them; I recounted to
her the whole story which I had just learned and
which she would have listened to more attentively
had not her equanimity been disturbed by a bad two-
franc piece which the coal man had contrived to
palm off on her that very day.

The *De Viris* gave me some further delights. I
fell in love with the nymph Egeria who, in a grotto

beside a fountain, inspired Numa with wise laws.
But soon I had the whole crowd of Sabines, Etrus-
cans, Latins and Volscians on my hands, and they
were more than I could tackle. And, then, if my
French was small my Latin was nil. One day M.
Grépinet put me on to construe a passage in this
obscure *De Viris*, something about the Samnites. I
showed myself totally incapable of performing the
task, and was reprimanded before the whole class.
I thereupon conceived a mortal disgust for the *De
Viris* and the Samnites. Nevertheless, my soul was
filled with wonder when I remembered Rhea Silvia
on whom a god bestowed two children who were
taken from her and suckled by a wolf amid the rushes
of the Tiber.

The superior, M. l'Abbé Meyer, was attractive
by reason of his gentleness and distinguished appearance. I still remember him as a prudent, affectionate
and motherly sort of man.

He used to dine in the refectory at eleven o'clock
with all the boys, and ate his salad with his fingers.
I do not say this in order to defame his memory.
In his young days, that used to be quite the correct
thing. My Aunt Chausson assured me that my
uncle never ate his lettuce in any other way.

The Director often came to see us while M.
Grépinet was taking his class. He signed to us, as he
entered, to keep our seats and, then, passing along in
front of the desks, he examined each boy's work. I

did not notice that he paid less attention to me than
to my richer or more aristocratic fellow pupils. He
spoke to us with a graciousness that was especially
noticeable when he had occasion to find fault with us,
and his reproaches did not crush our spirits. He did
not magnify our faults, he did not question our good
intentions. His admonitions were as innocent and
slight as the delinquencies which provoked them.
He told me one day that I wrote like a cat. The
comparison was a novel one to me and it sent me
off into fits of laughter, which became more than ever
uncontrollable when, in order to show me how to
form one's letters, he picked up my pen that only
had half a nib to it, and wrote like a cat indeed.

From that day forth M. le Directeur never once
passed by my desk without enjoining me to look
after my pens, not to dig them right down into the
inkpot, and always to wipe them when I had done
with them.

"A pen ought to last a long time," he added one
day. "I know of a great scholar who only used one
pen to write a whole book as big as—" And casting his eye round the bare room he spread out his
arms and indicated the great red marble chimney-
piece.

I was lost in wonderment.

A little while afterwards, as I was walking with
Justine along the Rue du Vieux-Colombier, I noticed,
in a yard in front of an antique dealer's, a stone saint

so huge that his head reached up to the first floor windows. He was writing in a book as big as a mantelpiece, with a pen to match. I informed my nurse that he was the friend of M. le Directeur, and she thought that well he might be.

If happiness did not regularly dwell with me, ecstasy was an occasional visitor. It frequently happened to me to become drunk with all the movement and noise that went on in the playground during one of the after-dinner breaks. In play as in work I could not put up with rules. I did not care about those geometrical games such as prisoner's base which had to be played strictly according to rule. Their exactitude bored me. They did not seem to me to give a picture of life. I liked the games detested by mothers, the games that the ushers used to put a stop to sooner or later because of the disorder they involved, games without rule or restraint, rough, furious games, full of horror.

Now, on that day, at the usual signal, we swarmed out into the playground. Hangard, our leader, who lorded it over us all by reason of his lofty stature, his big voice, and his masterful disposition, stood up on a stone seat and held forth.

Hangard stammered, but he was eloquent. He was an orator, a leader of men; there was something of the Camille Desmoulins in his composition.

"Look here, you kids," said he, "aren't you sick to death of playing 'puss in the corner' and 'leapfrog'? Let's have a change. Let's play at 'Robbing the Coach.' I'll show you how. It'll be jolly fine. You see if it won't."

We answered him with acclamations and shouts of joy. Suiting the action to the word, Hangard organized the game. His genius was equal to everything. In a trice the coach horses were put to, the postilions cracked their whips, the robbers armed themselves with knives and blunderbusses, the passengers strapped up their luggage and filled their purses and their pockets with gold. The gravel in the playground and the lilac bushes that enclosed the garden of M. le Directeur furnished the necessary accessories. Off we went. I was a passenger and one of the humblest; but my heart thrilled at the beauty of the landscape and the perils of the road. The robbers were lying in wait for us in the gorge of a fearful mountain—to wit the glass roof of the steps leading up into the parlour. The onslaught was swift and terrible. The postilions were knocked off their horses. I was bowled over, pounded with blows, buried under a heap of corpses. Standing erect on this human mountain, Hangard made a redoubtable fortress of it. Twenty times the robbers swarmed up it, twenty times they were hurled back again. I was beaten to a mummy; knees and elbows scraped raw, the tip of my nose incrusted with little bits of sharp grit, lips torn, ears aflame—never had I drunk in such delight. When the school bell rang and broke in upon my dream, my heart was rent in twain. All the time M. Grépinet was giving us our lesson, I sat dazed and devoid of feeling. My nose was smarting, my knees burning; but I liked the sensation because it recalled that crowded hour of glorious life. M. Grépinet asked me several questions which I was unable to answer. He called me a donkey, which was the more painful to me inasmuch as, not having read the *Metamorphoses*, I was as yet unaware that I only had to munch roses in order to recover my humanity. Learning it subsequently, when I had reached man's estate, I have lounged at leisure through the groves of Wisdom, feeding my donkey nature on the roses of science and meditation. I have devoured whole bushes, with their perfume and their thorns, but above my human head there would ever be pricking the tiniest tip of a pointed ear.

CHAPTER XXXII

VERY time I go into the Parc de Neuilly I am reminded of Clément Sibille, the gentlest soul, as it seems to me, of any that I ever saw skimming the surface of this terrestrial globe. He was, I think, nearing the end of his tenth year when I first made his acquaintance. I was a year older than he, but the superiority which my age gave me over him I wantonly threw away by my faults. The fates only suffered me to catch a momentary glimpse of him; yet now, though so many years have rolled by, I still seem to see him amid the foliage, through the railings, whenever I go into the Parc de Neuilly.

Monsieur and Madame Sibille had a house there, and in the summer I used to go with my father and mother to spend a few hours with them of a Sunday afternoon. Madame Sibille, whose Christian name was Hermance, was pale, slim and supple of limb. With her green eyes, prominent cheek-bones and small chin, she gave one a tolerably close impression of a cat that had been metamorphosed into a woman, with some of the characteristics of her former nature still clinging about her. Isidore Sibille, her husband, was an elongated, dismal looking person, and resembled a stork. It was thus that the couple appeared to my father, who, after the manner of Lavater, used to amuse himself by seeking in human countenances a likeness to members of the animal kingdom. From these resemblances he would deduce notions as to their character and temperament, but so vague and rash were his conclusions that I should be hard put to it to say precisely what he derived from these semblances of bird and cat. All I know about M. Sibille is that he was manager of a big French cashmere factory. I have heard my mother say that the Empress Eugénie sometimes wore these cashmeres for the sake of encouraging home industries, and that this was one of the most unwelcome duties that could devolve upon a sovereign, so painful were these cashmeres to behold. It was observed that Hermance herself always refrained from wearing them.

The Sibilles' house, in the Parc de Neuilly, was a white one, flanked by a turret. In front, a flight of steps led up from a beautiful lawn in the middle of which was a fountain surrounded by a stone basin. It was here, on the garden paths, that, frail and seemingly ever about to take flight heavenward, there first dawned on my view Clément Sibille. His eyes were of a limpid blue, his complexion a dazzling white, his features of extraordinary delicacy. His fair hair was cut very close to his round head, but his ears, so far from lying back against the temporal bone, were at right angles to it, and stuck out on either side of his head like a couple of flags that by a curious freak of nature were so shaped as to resemble the wings of a butterfly. They were transparent and, when the light shone through them, took on colours of pink and carmine, and glowed with dazzling hues. You did not realize that they were big ears; you thought you were looking at miniature wings. At all events that is the picture my memory conjures up. Clément was very pretty, but he was odd.

"Clément's got butterfly's wings," I said.

And my mother answered:

"Painters and sculptors portray Psyche after the same fashion with butterfly wings, and Psyche was taken to wife by Eros and admitted into the assembly of the gods and goddesses."

One more learned than I in mythological lore might have retorted that Psyche did not wear her wings at the side of her head in the place where her ears ought to be.

Clément was an unsubstantial fairy thing. He progressed by little leaps, not in a direct line but casting himself from side to side as though he were the sport of the winds. The simplicity of his amusements, his childish ways, and the infantile awkwardness of his movements, were in pathetic contrast with the kindness of his disposition, which was of

a strength and a manly staunchness that seemed to
suggest a person of riper years. His soul was as
transparent and pure as his complexion, as serene
and untroubled as his expression. He spoke but
little and always affectionately. He never complained, though he had perpetual reason to complain.
Diseases were only too ready to seek a lodging
within his puny frame, and scarlet fever, typhoid,
measles, whooping cough followed each other in
rapid succession. And perhaps a malady then but
little understood, tuberculosis, had gained access to
his narrow chest. Even when illness allowed
him a respite, Fate did not let him off. He met with
accidents so extraordinary in their nature and so
frequent in their occurrence, that it seemed as though
some invisible power were cunningly devising means
to persecute him. But all these misfortunes redounded
to his advantage in that they afforded him opportunities to display his unalterable gentleness. He was
for ever slipping, stumbling, tripping in every con-
ceivable and inconceivable manner, butting into every
wall, pinching his fingers in every door, so that he
was perpetually growing fresh nails. He cut himself sharpening his pencils, he got a bone in his
throat from every fish that lake, pond, brook,
stream, river or sea produced for him and that Malvina, the Sibilles' cook, prepared for his nourish-
ment. His nose would begin to bleed just as he was
going to see Robert Houdin or to have a donkey-ride

in the Bois de Boulogne and, despite the key they put down the back of his neck, he would stain his new waistcoat and his beautiful white knickerbockers. One day—I saw the thing happen before my very eyes—he was whirling round and round on the lawn, when he went and tumbled right into the fountain. Being afraid lest he should take a chill or get a cold on the chest, his people did everything they could think of to warm him up; I saw him in bed with a monster eiderdown on the top of him, a baby's bonnet on his head, and a seraphic smile on his countenance. When he saw me he begged my pardon for leaving me all alone with nothing to do.

I had no brother, no playmate with whom to compare myself. When I beheld Clément, I discovered that Nature had bestowed on me a restless spirit, tumultuous longings, a heart fulfilled of vain desire and unreasoning sorrow. Nothing availed to mar the tranquillity of his soul. If I failed to learn from him that whether we are happy or unhappy depends on ourselves alone, I only had myself to blame. But I was deaf to lessons on good conduct. Well had it been for me had I not provided, in contrast to good little Clément, the very type of a child who loved rough play, a harum-scarum mischievous urchin. Such a child was I, and as such the world considered me. Must I plead, in my own justification, that my actions were ordered by that mysterious power, that dread Necessity, who imposes her laws

alike on gods and men and who governed my actions even as she governs the universe. Am I to
plead that it was the love of Beauty that inspired
me then even as it has inspired me all the days of
my life, whereof it has been alike the torment and
the joy. Wherefore should I do so? When was
a man ever judged by the canons of natural philosophy and the laws of æsthetics. But let me state the
facts.

One autumn afternoon Clément and I were
given leave to go for a walk by ourselves on the
boulevard in front of the Sibilles' house. This boulevard was not then disfigured by long lines of monotonous railings shutting off the gardens. It was more
countrified in those days, more mysterious, and more
beautiful. Dead leaves floated down from the tall
trees like flakes of light and strewed the ground
beneath our feet. Clément was skipping along a few
paces in front of me, and I noticed that his black
cloth cap trimmed with dark red braid, an ugly
shaped, ugly coloured thing, came right down over
his pretty little golden curls and pressed back the
wonderful appendages that served him for ears. I
did not like that cap. I was ill advised enough not
to keep my eyes off it, and the thing got more and
more on my nerves. At last I could stand it no
longer, and I asked my companion to take it off.
Doubtless he regarded the request as unreasonable,
since he did not trouble to reply but serenely con-

tinued his pirouetting. Again I told him peremp-
torily to remove his cap.

Taken aback at my persistence, he mildly inquired:

"Why?"

"Because it's ugly."

He thought I was jesting, but all the same he kept
an eye on me, and when I tried to pull it off he re-
sisted my attempt and pressed his cap down on his
head with care and caution, for he loved his cap
and deemed it a thing of beauty. Twice more I essayed to gain possession of the odious headgear.
Each time he pressed it farther down on his head
and made it more odious still. Thus foiled, I suspended my attacks, but I had a dodge at the back
of my mind. His pretty face, whereon was written
a look of pained surprise, soon recovered its habitual
expression of tranquil innocence. How could I have
failed to be touched by his look of unsuspecting
trust? Alas, the spirit of violence was within me.
Watching my opportunity, I suddenly rushed at him,
laid hold of the cap, and sent it flying over the wall
into Louis Philippe's park.

Clément said not a word, he uttered not a cry.
He just looked at me with wondering, reproachful
eyes that cleft my heart in twain, and his eyes glistened with tears. I stood there as though trans-
fixed, unable to realize that I had done so criminal
a deed, and on the winged and curly head of Clément

I still sought the form of that ill-fated cap. It was there no more; it had vanished beyond recall. The wall was very high, the park vast and deserted. The sun was near to setting. Fearful lest Clément should catch cold or, rather, distressed at the sight of his bare head, I covered it with my own Tyrolese hat, which descended right over his eyes and dismally bent down his ears. In silence we made our way back to the Sibilles' house. I need not describe the reception I got.

That was the last time my parents took me to call on their Neuilly friends. I never saw Clément again. Poor little person, he soon afterwards vanished from this world. His butterfly wings waxed larger and larger, and, when they were strong enough to bear him, he flew away. His grief-stricken mother essayed in vain to follow him. The kindly gods metamorphosed her into a cat, and, uttering her doleful plaint, she looks for him over the house-tops.

CHAPTER XXXIII

A DIGRESSION

HAVE already used up a good deal of paper with these recollections of my early days, but I have just found, tucked away in a corner of my memory, something my mother said about me when I was quite a little boy. One day she was going to take me for a walk, and she spent what seemed to me an eternity in getting ready. When at last she appeared, looking so nice and so happy, I glanced at her sullenly, so at least I am told, and declared that I would not go for that walk, or for any other walk, and that I renounced all the pleasures and all the good things of this world, from that day forth and for evermore.

"Oh, dear! What a temper the child has," sighed my mother.

I did not think it was quite right of her to say that, in spite of what had led up to it. It is true that when I came to examine myself in comparison with my well behaved little friend whom the gods changed into a butterfly, I freely recognized that I was not gentle, not placid as he was. And, to be

quite frank about it, my desires being more ardent
than those of most children, I capitulated more
promptly to Necessity. From my earliest years,
Reason exercised a potent sway over me. That
means that I was an exceptional creature, for it is
not the case with the majority of my kind. Of all
the ways of defining man, I think the worst is the
one which makes him out to be a reasoning animal.
It is no great boast on my part to set myself up
as a being endowed with a larger share of reason
than most of those whom I have met or heard about.
Reason rarely dwells in common minds but still more
rarely in great ones. I say "reason," and if you
inquire in what sense I employ the term, I reply
in the everyday sense. If I attached a metaphysical
signification to it, I should not know what I meant
myself. I apply the same meaning to it as old Mélanie, who did not know her letters. I call a reasonable man a man who makes his own particular
mind so to square with the mind universal that he
is never unduly surprised at anything that happens,
and manages to accommodate himself to circumstances more or less successfully. I call that man
reasonable who, observing the lack of order that ex-
ists in the natural world and the folly of mankind,
does not persist in talking of the order of the one,
and the wisdom of the other. In a word, I call him
reasonable who does not make too self-conscious an
effort to appear so.

I fancy I was such a one. But, upon my word, when I come to think about it, I don't know, and I don't want to know. An unbeliever in the wisdom of the Delphic oracle, far from endeavouring to know myself, it has been my constant endeavour to do the very opposite. I hold the knowledge of one-self to be a source of care, anxiety and distress. I have had as little commerce as possible with my-self. It seemed to me that wisdom lay in turning away from the contemplation of oneself, in forget-ting one's own existence, or in imagining oneself to be different, by nature and fortune, from what one really is. Know not thyself; that is the beginning of wisdom.

If it be true that Montaigne composed his Es-says in order to study his own personality, his re-searches must have caused him more anguish than the stones which rent his kidneys. I think, on the contrary, that he wrote his book to distract his thoughts from, rather than to concentrate them on, the contemplation of his own individuality.

And let it not be said that this sermon on self-forgetfulness is singularly out of place in a book where the writer's self is his sole theme. I am a different person from the child I am writing about. We have nothing in common now, not a grain of substance, not a grain of thought. Now that he has become a total stranger, I am enabled to find in his company some relief from my own. I, who neither hate nor love myself, love him. It is pleas-ant to live over again in thought the days he lived. The very air of these present times is painful to breathe.

CHAPTER XXXIV

THE COLLEGIAN

T was the first day of term. I had spent a certain length of time at St. Joseph's, where I used to construe the *Epitome* to an accompaniment of twittering sparrows, and I was now to attend the college as a day boy.

I was, then, a collegian. I felt the honour, but with some anxiety, for I feared it would be a weighty one. I hadn't the slightest wish to cut a brilliant figure on those ink-stained forms, and when I was ten I had no ambitions. And, furthermore, I had no hopes. At the preparatory school I had been noted for a perpetual look of wonderment, and, rightly or wrongly, that is not regarded as a mark of very great intelligence. I was indeed looked upon as just a little simple. That was an injustice. I was as intelligent as the majority of my comrades, but I was intelligent in a different manner. Their intelligence served them in the ordinary circumstances of life; mine only came to my aid in the rarer and more unlooked-for conjunctures. It manifested itself unexpectedly in wanderings far afield or in a

liking for reading things out of the ordinary run. I
had given up the idea of distinguishing myself in
class, and from the day I entered the college I set
about getting what distraction I could out of my
new surroundings. Such was my nature and my bent,
and I have never changed. I have always known
how to amuse myself. For me, that comprised the
whole art of living. Little and big, young and
old, I have always lived as far as possible away
from myself and away from the tristful reality of
things. And so, on this first day of term, I was conscious of a desire to escape from my environment
that was all the keener because that environment
struck me as peculiarly uninviting. The college was
ugly, dirty, and evil-smelling, my classmates disagreeable and the masters depressing. Our form master looked at us without enthusiasm and without affection, and he was neither sufficiently sensitive nor
sufficiently insincere to put on the semblance of a
regard which he did not feel. He did not harangue
us. He merely surveyed us for a moment, and then
asking us our names, entered them, as we called them
out, in a big register that lay open on his desk. I
thought him old and machine-like, but I daresay he
was not as old as I thought him. When he had
taken down our names, he ruminated on them for
some time in silence, so as to assimilate them thoroughly. I believe that he got hold of them all immediately. He had learnt from experience that a

master has no hold on his boys, unless he is familiar with their names and faces.

"I will call out the names of the books you will need and which you must get as quickly as you can," he said.

Thereupon he proceeded to enumerate in monotonous drawling tones a number of forbidding titles such as lexicons and rudiments (why cannot these things be introduced to little children by more attractive names?), the Fables of Phædrus, an arithmetic, a geography, the *Selectæ e Profanis,* and so on and so forth. And then he wound up with something I had never heard of before: *Esther* and *Athalie.*

Forthwith there arose before my eyes, in a sort of blissful haze, two graceful female figures, attired as one sees in pictures, their arms encircling each other's waist, exchanging words that I could not hear, but that I divined were full of grace and charm. The master, and the master's chair, the blackboard, the drab walls, had all disappeared. The two women were walking slowly along a narrow path through fields of wheat a-bloom with cornflowers and poppies, and their names fell like music on my ears: Esther and Athalie.

I knew, without being told, that Esther was the elder. She had a kind heart. Athalie, who was not so tall, had, as far as I could make out, fair hair hanging down in plaits. They dwelt in the country. I seemed to descry a hamlet, thatched roofs with smoke curling upwards, a shepherd, and villagers joining in the dance. But all the features in the picture remained undefined, and I was all eagerness to learn what happened to Esther and to Athalie. The master calling out my name rudely dispelled my dreams.

"Are you going to sleep? You're wool-gathering. Come, now, pay attention and take down what I tell you."

The master began to call out the homework for the next day. There was a Latin exercise to be done, and one of Fénelon's fables to prepare.

When I got home, I gave my father the list of books which I was supposed to get as soon as possible. My father quietly read it through and told me I must obtain the books from the college bursar.

"By so doing," he said, "you will get the edition adopted by your masters and used by most of the other boys in your form; same text, same notes. That will be far the best way."

And he gave me back the list.

"But," said I, "how about *Esther and Athalie?*"

"Well, my boy, the bursar will give you *Esther* and *Athalie* when he gives you the other books."

I was disappointed. I should have liked to have *Esther and Athalie* right away. I counted on getting a deal of pleasure therefrom. I kept hovering round the table where my father was busy writing.

"Papa, *Esther and Athalie?*"

"Don't waste your time. Get on with your work and leave me alone."

I wrote out my Latin exercise, squatting on one heel. I did it without relish and I did it badly.

During dinner my mother put several questions to me regarding the masters, the other boys, and the classes.

I told her that my master was old and dirty, that he blew his nose like a trumpet, and that he was always strict and sometimes unfair. As for the boys, some I praised up to the skies, others I as inordinately decried. I had no feeling for the finer shades, and I was unwilling as yet to recognize the all-pervading mediocrity of men and things.

"It's nice, isn't it, *Esther and Athalie?*" I inquired of my mother all of a sudden.

"Very nice; but they are two plays," replied my mother.

I looked so blank as she said this that my excellent mother deemed it behoved her to explain the matter with great precision.

"They are two separate plays, dear, two tragedies; *Esther* is one play, *Athalie* is another."

Thereupon, with great seriousness, calmness, and determination, I said:

"They're not."

My mother in amazement asked me how I could contradict her in such a rude, silly manner.

I persisted in my denial, and said that they were not two plays. *Esther and Athalie* was a single story, and I knew it. Esther was a shepherdess.

"Very well, then," said my mother. "It is an *Esther and Athalie* I know nothing about. You must let me see the book in which you have read this story."

I maintained a gloomy silence for some moments, and then with a heart overflowing with bitterness and melancholy I said again:

"I tell you that *Esther and Athalie* are not two plays."

My mother was endeavouring to convince me, when my father angrily told her to take no notice of me if I persisted in being so opinionated and pigheaded.

"He's taken leave of his senses," he added.

And my mother heaved a sigh. I saw—I see it still—her bosom rise and fall beneath the black taffeta bodice that was fastened at the neck with a little gold brooch in the shape of a knot, with two little trembling tassels dangling from it.

Next morning, at eight o'clock, Justine, my maid, took me to school. I had some cause for misgiving. My Latin exercise did not satisfy me and seemed to me very unlikely to satisfy anybody else. The mere look of it betokened a scamped and a faulty piece of work. The writing, which was careful and fine enough to begin with, got rapidly worse as it went on, and finally degenerated into an ungainly scrawl. But I rammed my anxiety well down into the obscure depths of my being. I drowned it. When I was ten I was wise at least on one point. I deemed it useless to repine over the irreparable, and thought that, as Malherbe says, we ought not to seek a remedy for an irremediable misfortune, to repent a fault being merely adding to one evil another more grievous still. We must forgive ourselves a deal of things if we would accustom ourselves to forgiving others. Thus I forgave myself my Latin exercise. As I passed by the grocer's shop, I caught sight of some candied fruits gleaming in their boxes like gems in a white velvet jewel-case. The cherries were rubies, the angelica emeralds, the plums giant topazes, and since, of all the senses, it is sight that procures me the strongest impressions, the view of them straightway seduced me, and I bewailed the lack of means that prevented me from acquiring one of those boxes. The smallest was one and threepence. If repentance held no sway over me, desire has ruled the whole course of my life. I may, indeed, say that my life has been one prolonged desire. I love desire; I love the joys and pangs of desire. To desire with ardour is almost like to possession. Nay—what am I saying?—it is possession, without satiety or disgust. Nevertheless, can I aver with confidence that, when I was a child of ten, I thus philosophized about desire, and that I

held these tenets in their complete and finished form?
I would not stake my life on that; nor am I prepared to swear that, in after years, the sting of desire has not sometimes been so keen as to cause me
pain beyond endurance. Well had it been for me had
I never set my heart on anything but boxes of candied
fruits.

I used to live on the friendliest terms with
Justine. I was affectionate, she was lively. I loved
her without feeling that I was loved by her in return, a thing which, if the truth must be told, is a
little foreign to my character.

That morning we were walking along on our way
to the college, each holding on to the strap of my
satchel and giving, now and again, little sudden
sharp tugs that might have pulled us over if we
had been less firm on our feet. As a rule, I handed
on to Justine all the harsh and even insulting things
that had been said to me during the day. I questioned her on difficult subjects, even as I myself
had been questioned. She either did not answer
or else she answered wrong, and I said to her
what I had had said to me: "You are an ass. You
shall have a bad mark. Aren't you ashamed of your
laziness?" Thus it happened that on that particular morning, I asked her whether she knew *Esther
and Athalie.*

"Esther and Athalie, mon petit monsieur? But
those are just names."

"Justine, you deserve to be kept in for answering like that."

"They *are* names, mon petit maître. Natalie is my foster-sister's name."

"I daresay it is, but you haven't read the story of Esther and Athalie. No, you haven't read it. Well, I am going to tell it you."

And I told it:

"Esther was a farmer's wife at Jouy-en-Josas. One day, as she was walking in the country she came across a little girl who had fainted from weariness by the roadside. She brought her round, gave her some bread and some milk, and asked her name."

I continued the narrative until we reached the college gates. And I was sure that the story was true, and that I should find it set down exactly like that in my book. You ask how I arrived at that conclusion. I cannot say. But I was quite sure of it. This day was not at all memorable. My exercise went through unnoticed, and disappeared obscurely like the great multitude of human actions which hurry by into the darkness and leave no memory behind them. Next morning I found myself possessed with a mighty enthusiasm for Binet. Binet was a little thin person with sunken eyes, a big mouth, and a grating voice. He wore little black patent-leather boots with white stitching. He dazzled me. The universe melted away before my

eyes; I beheld but Binet. I can discover no reason
for my enthusiasm when I come to look back over
the matter now, except those same patent-leather
boots, which spoke so eloquently of the pride and
elegance of a bygone day. If you deem the reason a
trifling one, then I say that the history of man will
for ever remain a sealed book to you. When we
speak of the Greeks, are they not essentially known
to us as the well-greaved Greeks?

The next day, Wednesday, was a holiday,
and it was not until the Thursday that we got
our books from the bursar. He made us sign
a receipt which gave us a great idea of our importance as members of the civil community. We
inhaled our books with delight. They smelt of
paper and glue. They were quite new. We wrote
our names on the title page. Some of us made a
blot on the cover of a grammar, maybe, or a dic-
tionary, and were exceeding sorrowful. Nevertheless, it was fated that these books were to receive
inkstains more numerous than the splashes of mud
on the windows of the grocer's shop in the Rue des
Saints-Pères in winter. The first stain was dreadful; the others followed as a matter of course. These
considerations suggest a train of thought which, if
pursued, would carry us far from grammars and
dictionaries. For my part, I searched forthwith in
my packet of books for *Esther and Athalie*. Howbeit, by a stroke of ill-fortune which wounded me to

the quick, that work was lacking. I spoke to the
bursar about it. He said that I need not worry, that
I should have it all in good time.

It was not until a fortnight later, All Souls' Day,
that I got *Esther* and *Athalie*. It was a little volume
bound in boards and backed with blue linen. A grey
paper label on the cover gave the title as follows:
Racine, *Esther* and *Athalie*, Tragedies Founded on
Holy Writ and Edited for the Use of Schools. That
title boded nothing good in my eyes. I opened the
book. It was worse than the gloomiest forebodings
could have suggested. *Esther* and *Athalie* were poetry. Now every one knows that things written in
poetry are hard to understand and uninteresting.
Esther and *Athalie* were two separate plays and all
in verse, and long verses, at that. Alas, my mother's
words had come too cruelly true! So Esther was not
a farmer's wife, and Athalie was not a little beggar
maiden. Esther had not come upon Athalie by the
wayside. So I had been dreaming. And what a
charming dream! And how dismal and wearisome
the reality compared with my reverie! I shut the
book and vowed I would never open it again. I did
not keep my word.

O great and tender-hearted Racine! best and dearest of poets! in such wise did I first make acquaintance with you. You are now my love and my delight.
In you lies all my happiness, my dearest joy. It
was little by little, as I went forward in life, slowly

gaining experience of men and things, that I learned
to know you and to love you. Compared with you
Corneille is but a skilful rhetorician, and I know not
if even Molière himself is so true to life as you, O
sovereign master, with whom all truth abides, all
beauty! When I was young and misled by the precepts and examples of those barbarous romanticists,
I did not at first perceive that you were the pro-
foundest, even as you were the purest, of all tragic
poets. My eyes were not strong enough to contemplate your splendour. I have not always spoken
of you with sufficient admiration. I have neglected
to say that the characters created by you were the
truest that poet ever conjured forth into the light
of day. I have left it unrecorded that you were very
life and very nature. You alone have made real
women tread the stage. What are the women of
Sophocles and Shakespeare beside the women whom
you have animated with the breath of life? They
are but puppets. None but yours know love and
desire; the others do but talk. I would not willingly
die without graving a few lines at the foot of your
monument, O Jean Racine, in witness of my love
and veneration, but if the time to perform this sacred
duty be not vouchsafed me, then let these lines,
casual but sincere, betoken what is in my heart.

But wait. I have not recorded that, having refused to learn Esther's prayer: *O mon souverain
roi* (the noblest lines in the French language) my

form master made me write out fifty times the verb:·
"I have not learnt my lesson." He was a profane
mortal. It is not so that we avenge the glory of a
poet. To-day I know my Racine by heart, and he is
ever new to me. As for you, old Richou (such was
my master's name), I loathe your memory. You
profaned the poetry of Racine when you spouted it
from your thick lips. The sense of harmony was not
in you. You deserved the fate of Marsyas. I deem
that I did well to refuse to learn *Esther,* so long as
I was under your sway. But you, Maria Favart,
you, Sarah, you, Bartet, you, Weber, may the benison
of heaven descend upon you, for that you distilled
from your lips divine, like honey and ambrosia, the
music of *Esther,* of *Phèdre,* and of *Iphigénie.*

CHAPTER XXXV

MY ROOM

 BELLAGUET continued till his dying day to enjoy the esteem which is the customary prerogative of prosperous dishonesty. His grateful family bore him to the grave in solemn state. Prominent financiers acted as pall-bearers. Behind the hearse, the master of the ceremonies carried a cushion on which were displayed the insignia of the various orders—crosses, ribbons, medals and badges and stars—that had been granted to the deceased.

As the procession passed along, women crossed themselves, the men in the crowd took their hats off and murmured under their breath such words as "sharper," "swindler," and "old rogue," reconciling in this way their respect for the dead with their sense of justice.

Having entered into possession of the deceased's estate, his heirs had several changes carried out in the house, and my mother persuaded them to have our flat rearranged and done up. By making a few alterations and doing away with some dark closets and cupboards, they managed to construct an-

other little room, which was allotted to me. Up to
then I had slept either in a sort of slip-room adjoining the drawing-room which was too small for the
door to be shut at night, or else in the dressing-room,
which was already chock-full of furniture. And I
used to do my homework on the dining-room table.
Justine would come and unceremoniously interrupt
my studies in order to lay the cloth and the substi-
tution of plates, dishes, knives and forks, for books,
paper, and writing materials was always attended by
a breach of the peace. But when I got a room of
my own I did not know myself. A child the day before, I suddenly became a young man. My ideas
and tastes suddenly sprang into being. Henceforth,
I lived my own life. I possessed an individual existence.

The view from my room was neither pleasant nor
extensive. It looked out on a back yard. The wall-
paper displayed a field of blue blossoms on a cream-
coloured background. The furniture consisted of a
bed, two chairs, and a table. The cast iron bedstead
is worthy of being described in some detail. It was
painted in a colour that was not selected with a due
regard to the circumstance that the bed was supposed to imitate violet ebony. It was ornamented
throughout in the style of the Renaissance, as that
style was customarily interpreted in the days of
Louis Philippe, and the forepart especially was conspicuous for a medallion adorned with pearls, from

which there stood out in relief a woman's head with a band round her hair. The head and foot of the bed were embellished with figures of birds and foliage. It must be borne in mind that all these objects, the woman's head, the birds, and the foliage, were in cast iron designed to imitate violet ebony. How my poor mother ever came to buy such a thing was a cruel mystery that I never had the courage to fathom. At the foot of the bed was a strip of carpet with a pattern representing some little children playing with a dog. On the walls hung water-colour drawings of Swiss women in national costume. Besides the articles of furniture already mentioned, there were a set of shelves on which I used to put my books, a walnut cabinet, and a little Louis XVI rosewood table that I would gladly have exchanged for my godfather's roll-top mahogany desk, which, in my estimation, would have made me look more important.

As soon as I got a room to myself, I began to live a life of my own; I was conscious of an inward existence. I became capable of reflexion, of retiring into my own soul. As for my room, I did not look on it as beautiful. I never thought for a moment that it ought to be. Nor did I think it ugly. I just looked upon it as unique, incomparable. It fenced me about from the universe, and within it I found the universe again.

It was there that my mind was formed, there that

it broadened out and began to people itself with phantoms. Poor little room of my childhood days, it was within your four walls that there began slowly to gather round me the many hued shadows of knowledge, all those illusions that have hidden nature from my sight and gathered more and more densely between myself and her as I increased my efforts to unveil her mystery. It was there, within your four narrow walls, with their garlands of blue flowers, that there appeared to me, at first faint and far-off, the terrifying simulacra of Love and Beauty.

THE END

it broadened out and began to people itself with phantoms. Poor little room of my childhood days, it was within your four walls that there began slowly to gather round me the many hued shadows of knowledge, all those illusions that have hidden nature from my sight and gathered more and more densely between myself and her as I increased my efforts to unveil her mystery. It was there, within your four narrow walls, with their garlands of blue flowers, that there appeared to me, at first faint and far-off, the terrifying simulacra of Love and Beauty.

THE END